# WILDACRE

# ALSO BY SHANI STRUTHERS

# WILDACRE

## A CHRISTMAS GHOST STORY

## SHANI STRUTHERS

# Acknowledgements

A huge thank you to my core team of beta readers, Kate Jane Jones, Lesley Hughes, and Sarah Savery – your input and enthusiasm for Wildacre was, as usual, invaluable. Also to Louise Grassi for helping me fix a plot hole in a coffee shop in Brighton on a rainy day – the panic that would have ensued otherwise! Further thanks to my editor, Sue, for polishing the manuscript to perfection with her brilliant editing skills and to Gina Dickerson of RoseWolf Design for always knocking it out of the ballpark with yet another fantastic cover.

A very happy Christmas to one and all.

*Believe in the magic.*

# Chapter One

## *21st December*

"Jessica Lockhart, Jessica Lockhart. Where the hell are you, Jessica Lockhart?"

Northumberland was so barren in places. The least populated county in England, apparently, and Isla Barrow could well believe it. She'd left Alnwick, where she currently lived, what seemed like an age ago, to venture into the countryside, deep into it, to Jessica Lockhart's address, and had barely seen another soul on the road since.

In the silence of her car, the *echoing* silence, Isla sighed. Then again, who'd be on the road in weather like this? It was winter. December. A *dreich* day, as the neighbouring Scots would call it. What little light there'd been was fading rapidly, the night settling in, and with it a breeze that was picking up, the first spots of rain falling.

Not a long journey from Alnwick – forty-two miles – but the twisting, turning nature of the roads, along with the weather, meant progress was slow, and she'd be later than expected. Nothing she could do about that. No reason to keep fretting. She'd get there when she could. A barren land, she thought again, and in such a wild expanse, Jessica Lockhart. A woman in her eighties, whose last live-in carer had suddenly quit, and so close to Christmas too.

Subsequently, Isla had put her name forward, and got the gig.

Fed up of the silence in her car, Isla turned on the radio. Immediately, she wished she hadn't. *Merry Xmas Everybody*, a Slade classic, was being played, probably on an hourly loop, or half-hourly knowing her luck. If only she could reach her phone, currently in her rucksack on the backseat, and plug in one of her Spotify playlists. She should have thought to do that before she'd set off. Normally she did, but stuff was on her mind lately, more so than usual, the time of year perhaps responsible for that – a *poignant* time. And so, as soon as she'd got details of her new client, she stuffed some clothes and a few toiletries into a bag, and almost ran to her car on the street outside her flat. A change of scene. To be kept busy. It was a gift indeed.

*A change of scene.* She almost laughed at that, right along with the radio presenter, who was now speaking in between tracks. So much jollity in his voice, such…festivity. She'd had a change of scene only recently! She wasn't from Alnwick, but the south. A place she hadn't been for a long time. She just kept moving about, going from place to place, carers being needed everywhere. A nomad.

She glanced at the Sat Nav. Twenty-four more miles to go. Not far. Not really. But it was as though civilisation had been truly left behind. The rain on her windscreen was icy. It wasn't snowing yet, although in these parts snow wasn't exactly rare at this time of year. She couldn't see the countryside through the darkness. It was as though it had…disappeared. But she knew exactly what was out there. She'd travelled this way during her first weekend in Alnwick, to see it. That was during August, a far more clement season. The sight had taken her breath away.

She'd parked her car in a layby, climbed out and wandered in amongst grass and rockier terrain, eyes glued to all that surrounded her. An appreciation for the landscape was a relatively new acquisition in her armour. She'd clearly spent years blind to it. But this countryside was like no other. She loved the vastness of it, the drama, could sense how enduring it was, shadowy mountains set against an ever-changing sky. She was nothing in comparison. And she loved that too.

She hadn't been out here in recent months, though. She'd been kept too busy with work, with client after client in the town needing attention, the agency she worked for cramming her visits in, making a whirlwind of them. There was really only time to say and do what was absolutely necessary: get the client (the agency's term for it, not hers) out of bed, see to their personal care, make them breakfast, and leave it on the side for them to negotiate with frail hands that often shook. Then it was on to the next, and the next, microwaving some lunch or dinner, again leaving it on the side, praying they wouldn't choke on it. There were snatches of conversation, a few basic semantics observed, but that was all.

Lonely. That's what a lot of her clients were. Conversation being the thing they needed most, and Isla trying not to feel bad about that, guiltier than ever.

This time, though, with Jessica Lockhart, it'd be different. It was a live-in carer the woman needed, temporary cover, until the agency could fix up something more permanent in the New Year. They'd have plenty of time to get to know each other.

She checked the Sat Nav, the miles continuing to disappear. The house was called Wildacre. Fancy! Was

Jessica Lockhart a woman of means? She lived just outside Jedburgh, a further ten miles away. Not that far from civilisation really.

So why did it feel so lonely? As bleak as the people she visited. As…hopeless.

*Because of the darkness, of course. It makes everything worse.*

Something she knew all too well, having endured many sleepless nights.

Silence resumed as she turned the radio off, unable to stand more jingles being pumped out. And although it was an intense silence, it was preferable.

The miles kept dissolving, the road ahead kept twisting and turning, icy beads still falling from a blackened sky. There were some houses en route, a few that sat by the roadside, others reached via driveways, and no doubt stuffed with family.

Happy families? Perhaps there were young parents with little kids, those kids counting down the numbers on their advent calendars to the big day, when the man himself came to visit – Santa. If you were good, that is. If not, you got nothing.

She used to love Christmas. As a kid, she'd also counted down the days. Now, though, she was numb to it, or trying to be. As with last year, it was to be like any other day, something to get through. Luckily, in her line of work, as busy as any other time. A carer. Ironic, really, she'd ended up in that profession. A certain…cruelty to it.

What would *this* Christmas Day be like? In Wildacre, with Jessica Lockhart. Two strangers assigned to each other. It was a pretty name the woman had: slightly dreamy, romantic even, but maybe a misnomer if the other carer had left so hurriedly. Was she in actual fact a cantankerous old cow? Whatever the case was, how come she'd ended up so alone? Christmas was indeed a time for family, so had hers all moved away: sisters, brothers, daughters or sons? Or, as with so many that had grown old, was she deemed of no real value any more? Not until she died, that was, and her will was read: the spoils of a long life divided between vultures.

*You're being uncharitable, Isla!* And she duly chastised herself for it. She knew nothing about Jessica Lockhart, only that she needed help, that she was housebound, and could afford her, or rather the exorbitant fees the agency charged for 24/7 care. Isla wasn't squeamish, but she wondered how far personal care for Jessica would extend. The information she'd been provided with regarding her had been scant. It was Rog Ditton, one of the agency managers, who'd rung her about it. He'd been in a bar at the time, somewhere down in Newcastle – at a Christmas event, he'd said – and the line had been choppy.

He was drunk, although he was trying hard to disguise it. Isla could also tell he was pissed off in attitude too. No way he wanted his evening interrupted by work matters. Just as Jessica was alien to Isla, she was also alien to Rog. Just another client, another name on the books. Anonymous.

"Jess…Art…" he'd said. "Lives at…Acre. Paperwork emailed…morning. Okay?"

"Okay," Isla had replied, unable to resist adding, "So why did the other carer leave in such a hurry? I mean, like, is there something I should know?"

Laughter. Rog's and those of other revellers in the background.

"Sorry?" he'd said.

"I said," Isla raised her voice a little, "is there something I should know?"

5

"About what?"

"About her! Jessica. Is she like…difficult or something?"

"All in…paperwork," Rog had assured her. "Gotta go…bye."

What was in the paperwork, though, were merely the basics: Jessica's age, and the duties Isla should expect to carry out. She wasn't disabled, or at least not confined to a wheelchair. She was on the usual meds for her age, for her heart and blood pressure, that kind of thing, but she was vulnerable, out there on her own, her body having slowed down to a snail's pace, most likely, full of aches and pains. And if you could afford care, someone to wash and dress you, cook and clean, then why not? It suited Jessica, and right now, it suited Isla too. She'd be there from today, the 21st December, until around the 2nd or 3rd January, most likely. Then she'd return to her flat in Alnwick and just…carry on, working as many shifts as she could.

God, how different it was out here compared to Alnwick! There, each and every shopfront had been adorned with tinsel and decorations. LED lights had been hung from street lamp to street lamp in the town's square, and, as she'd left earlier this afternoon, people were hurrying along the streets carrying bulging bags. Later, the pubs, wine bars, and restaurants would all be heaving.

Out here, in such deep countryside, Christmas didn't seem to exist. No snow, just rain that was coming down harder – suddenly, and ferociously, the windscreen wipers doing their utmost to keep the way ahead clear.

Not long to go, though, a few more miles. Just over eight, the Sat Nav promised.

Such a relief to avoid more of the run-up to Christmas, seeing other people doing what she used to do: drinking too much and falling about the place, all in the name of fun. She was content to come out here, had actively wanted to, and yet now – because of the rain, surely? And how bad it was – nerves were creeping in. So dark before, visibility so reduced, and now there was this, weather which made the world smaller still. She had to lean forward in her seat and squint to see the road.

Eight miles now, soon that black chequered flag on the Sat Nav screen would appear, a voice that said "*You have reached your destination.*" She'd hurry into the house – the keys in an external key safe there, the combination given in the email, 0101 – and take a few moments to breathe before introducing herself to Jessica.

As she drove further, there were no more houses either side of the road, no chink of light from a living room or bedroom to signal another living being nearby.

She was the only one, focusing on the tunnel of road ahead.

Seven miles. Six. A hairpin bend, or at least it seemed like it in such darkness, something extreme. The Sat Nav showing a turnoff soon also worried her. This wasn't exactly a main road she was on, so how far off the beaten track did it want to take her? What led up to Wildacre? Little more than a dirt track?

*Calm down! Watch your breathing as well as the road!*

Okay, the night was as black as coal, and yes, the weather was getting worse, but she was almost there. Five miles to go, four-and-a-half… The bend was a bit before the three-mile marker, and it did indeed appear to be a one-way track, tall hedges either side making her feel even more hemmed in, claustrophobic. That command she'd just given herself about breathing easier was failing.

What if she should meet another car? How would they get around each other?

Before she could panic further, the road widened slightly.

"Thank fuck for that!"

It'd be okay. Another three miles or so and then she'd be in the warm and dry. She could settle Jessica, settle herself, climb into bed, and sleep. In the morning she'd get her bearings, because right now she had no clue where she was. She'd blindly followed the Sat Nav, placing her entire trust in it; trusting too that this situation with Jessica Lockhart would be okay, would be…routine. Wouldn't it?

"Shit!"

Was that traffic at last? A car in front of her, as she'd feared, the headlights just visible?

Her hands, already clutching the steering wheel hard, held on tighter as she swerved to the right, the car plummeting. Into what? A ditch?

"What's happening?"

It was a ditch! A deep one. There was a crunch too. Her body jerked back and forth, her head hit the backrest hard.

The car juddered to a halt, screeching like a banshee.

With echoing silence nothing but a mere memory, the furious beating of her heart drummed in her ears instead as icy rain continued to pelt the windows.

She'd crashed the car. Not even three miles from Wildacre. No other car on the road, although she'd been so sure… She had to reach her phone and call for help.

As she twisted her body round, she yelped, pain shooting up and down her spine. Sitting straight again, she tried a second time, each movement she made this time more tentative. The pain wasn't so intense, which she took as a good sign – no real damage done – although her hand was shaking hard as she grabbed at her rucksack.

Facing frontwards once more, she delved into it. Where was her mobile?

"Come on, come on, you're here somewhere!"

A few seconds later and she'd located it, hiding right at the bottom. She jabbed at the screen, and the glow it cast was eerie in such darkness. Holding down the buttons either side of the phone, the option to make an emergency call appeared. She slid the bar. Waited. When no connection was made, she tried a second, a third and a fourth time. Still no connection. No networks in the area available to latch onto.

Another scream erupting, she threw the mobile onto the seat beside her.

"Stupid, stupid thing," she yelled. "The Sat Nav worked, so why can't you?"

Tears sprang from her eyes, a torrent of them, her nose streaming as well.

She'd crashed, but she wasn't hurt. Not seriously. Was she?

Glad of something to do other than wail and curse, she checked herself, pressing at various bits of her body. The back of her head was certainly tender, but other than that, she was fine. Able to walk. No choice but to.

Wildacre was on this track, a few short miles away. She could be there inside an hour, probably. There had to be reception at the house, although she noticed that Rog had omitted to put a contact number for Jessica. This was typical of him; his mind was always elsewhere. As soon as she arrived, she'd call the emergency services, then Rog too, and to hell with it if he got narky about being disturbed. He was her point of contact, end of. *Just* them, she'd call. No friends, no family, to say something like '*Hey, you'll never guess what happened,*' and hear them reply, '*Oh, Isla! That's awful! You are okay, aren't you?*' Concern in their voice, such warmth.

More tears escaped her, which she angrily wiped at. There was no point in crying. Tears got you nowhere. She had to act. She couldn't stay here all night in the car or she'd freeze to death. Up ahead was a haven, a sanctuary. Wildacre. She had a feeling its name suited it, for this land in which it stood was indeed wild.

On another deep and shaky breath, she undid her seatbelt, groaning again at aches, real or imagined, as she reached for her mobile. God, she hoped Jessica didn't need too much care this evening. She just wanted to sink into bed and sleep. She felt overwhelmed with exhaustion, the shock of the crash clearly responsible.

Her phone back in her rucksack, she reached for the door and tried to open it. The wind pushed against her, making it an almost impossible task.

"Just…open…will you!"

The car being on its side slightly also made things difficult. Despite how she ached, the bruises that would eventually form, she persisted, and finally, it yielded.

As soon as her feet reached the ground, she stopped, her breath just too harsh. A little under three miles away, but it didn't matter. There was no way she could manage it. Too tired. Too shocked. Too much in pain.

Bloody weather! The breeze certainly had picked up, was more like a wind, and the icy rain was as sharp as needles on her face. Luckily, she hadn't packed much for her stay at Wildacre, and what she had could be washed and recycled easily enough. Her rucksack, once hauled into place, wouldn't weigh her down too much.

A short while later, and with a woolly hat pulled tight against her ears and a pair of gloves on her hands, she peered down the lane with renewed determination.

As it had in the car, the weather impaired her vision – the rain almost like curtains pulled tightly shut. The last house she'd seen had been around three miles back, so there was no point in going anywhere other than forwards.

She put one foot in front of the other.

"Okay, Jessica," she breathed, "and Wildacre, I'm coming for you."

# Chapter Two

## *21ˢᵗ December*

The lane widened, then narrowed, then widened. Despite not being able to see too far ahead, the light from her mobile barely cutting a swathe through the darkness, Isla had a sense it would go on for ever. The weather was merciless, icy beads clumping now on the ground, giving some definition at last to the shadows, cutting a clear line between hedgerow and sky when before there'd been none. She must have trudged a mile or more, cursing under her breath for most of that time, mad at herself for taking this job, and putting herself in such a precarious position.

*Always trying to escape. Always running away.*

And look where it had got her. Incredibly, she was worse off than before.

Fucking rain! It was so cold she felt like she was going to die. But would that be such a bad thing? She could hurl herself forwards into a ditch too, to lie there in the bracken, as abandoned as her car, growing colder and colder, until, eventually, her breath froze in her throat, and her heart refused to pump any more. Not such a bad ending. It didn't sound too painful. Then no more…shit. No more…guilt.

"Fuck it," she said, her foot catching in a pothole of some sort, almost causing her to topple over and add to her injuries.

Fully upright again, she glared at the ground just behind her, then sighed. As if a pothole would care if she threw it a dirty glance! She should look ahead, not backwards. Never any point in looking backwards. But God – it was as dark behind her as it was in front, and there she was, caught right in the middle.

"Not long to go," she muttered.

Not far. Twenty minutes, half an hour or so, time in which to do nothing but trudge. Just focus on a road that was indeed more of a dirt track, leading her even further away from civilisation than she was already. She had to live in the moment. No time to think. The last thing she wanted was to think, going over and over and over the nitty-gritty of past events, getting more upset, angrier. With whom? Herself or them?

*Both! Look what's happened to me because of it. It's not fair. None of this is!*

"GOD!" she screamed, a commotion of feathers and squawks accompanying her cry, which had startled some birds in a tree above her.

What a mistake this was, coming out here, into the middle of nowhere. Once she'd seen to the old lady, there'd be nothing to do but think! The best she could hope for was a dirty house, then she could scrub and scrub, making it gleam.

Wildacre sounded like a bit of a pile, and if Jessica Lockhart lived alone in it, then surely there'd be plenty of rooms that needed attention, dust that had built up, just begging to be removed. *Make it bright and shiny for the festive season!* Ha! What a task that would be, considering the last thing she felt was bright and shiny herself. But so what? You didn't have to feel it, to create it. It wasn't as if she was going to deck the halls with boughs of holly, hang tinsel everywhere, erect a bloody Christmas tree. She'd clean, and in that cleaning lose herself.

Then, after Wildacre, she'd go back to Alnwick, back on the treadmill, work, eat, sleep, rinse, repeat. *The dumbing-down of Isla Barrow, aged just twenty-four.* No meds required when sheer monotony did the trick.

Lost in thought, she also lost track of how far she'd come. Wiping the rain from her face, and sniffing hard, she squinted again. There! Not too far ahead, was a set of brick pillars – the kind you'd find at the beginning of a long driveway – with a pineapple or a round ball, cast in stone, sitting on top of them. As she drew closer, she saw they were indeed that, but plain, with ivy, a weed that grew unchecked, twisting around them. There was a heavy lean on one, as if it was about to collapse.

It was definitely an entrance to a driveway. Wildacre in her sights at last!

Isla picked up pace, not quite running – she was simply too tired, too achy – but walking as fast as she could, just so eager to be there.

Having reached the pillars she stopped, and looked further down the road.

This had to be it, despite there being no identifying plaque as far as she could tell.

She took a step forward, then stopped again.

It was dark inside the driveway. Darker than where she stood, the iciness of the rain lending no definition whatsoever. Shadows just…melted into each other, to form something more solid. *A wall of darkness.* Not inviting at all, but foreboding.

Earlier on the walk, she'd stuffed her mobile into her pocket, the light being so useless, opting to let her eyes adjust naturally to the darkness instead. Now, though, she reached for it and again jabbed at the screen.

It remained blank.

"Huh?"

She jabbed several more times. Shook it. Was it dead or something? Drained of charge? No way! There'd been plenty of charge in it when she'd left Alnwick. *The darkness has sucked the life from it.* A stupid thought, way too over the top. But out here, on this seemingly abandoned road, home to an abandoned house, with an abandoned woman in it, it was one that formed easily.

Just as she'd startled the birds in the tree earlier, the hoot of an owl startled her. She almost dropped the phone with fright.

*Pull yourself together, Isla! You're in a position of responsibility here.* And yet responsibility was the thing she'd proved herself the worst at.

She stuffed the phone back in her pocket, adjusted the backpack and began trudging up the driveway, the gravel beneath her feet crunching although it was also entangled with weeds, trees clashing against each other, delivering a resounding boom each time. Where the hell was this house? The trees as well as the rain obscured everything.

*Ridiculous. Fucking ridiculous.* This whole scenario was. When she was in the dry, in whatever bedroom she was allocated, she'd charge her phone, call Rog first actually, and get him to do the donkey-work regarding a vehicle recovery service. Maybe even suggest a job-share, if anyone else was insane enough to take it on, if perhaps whatever festive plans they'd made had fallen through. They could split the job straight down the middle, and she could return to Alnwick, sooner rather than later. Better to take her chances with the merriment on the street there, rather than whatever was here.

There was something up ahead at last. Not a house, though. Something other, to the left of the path. Something…pale.

From hurrying, she almost *skidded* to a halt.

Pale and…tall, about her height. Slimmer at the top, then becoming broader, as if…as if it was a figure of some sort. Two of them, actually. Three. One standing behind the other. Wearing cloaks?

She was shaking, and not just because she felt frozen through to the marrow, but because of *them*. Whatever *they* were.

She could shout out, yell something like, *Hey there, what are you doing? Do you…live here?* Her voice, though, had also frozen.

She couldn't turn back. There was *nothing* behind her! Only her useless car. Why weren't they moving? What were they doing, standing and staring?

Anger rose, and she welcomed it, coaxed it further. Weirdos! She'd march right up to them, *demand* to know their business. This was Christmas, not Halloween! She had to get to Wildacre. So whoever they were, they could clear off.

Kids, most likely. From a nearby house. Trying to have a little fun. God, how desperate could you be if you called this fun! Frolicking about in cloaks in the rain. Isla was only really used to city life. She came originally from Reading; not the best place in the world, but not the worst. It had decent shopping, plenty of pubs and bars. Did she miss it?

Not the town. There were better ones. The people, though…

Anger was really surging now as she broke into a stride. Anger at the past, at the present, and at *them*, those ahead that seemed to taunt her.

She'd face those kids, face them down. Put the fear of God into them instead.

*I'll teach you not to mess with me.*

She was closing the gap between them, her voice still stuck in her throat, but when it was unstuck, she wouldn't just shout, she'd bellow. *This is private property. Get out of here. Go back to wherever you've come from.*

Almost there, and her voice emerged, eventually. "Who are you?"

How could anyone stay that still? That silent?

Just a few feet away and she found out why, laughter bubbling upwards.

"Statues," the word burst from her.

Somehow, they'd caught whatever sliver of moonlight there was, to stand out against the darkness. Lidded urns. Nothing more sinister than that. And close up, they *looked* like urns, rather than demonic figures wearing Dracula-style capes. Funny how the dark distorted things. Just stone urns. Fancy indeed.

She reached out and touched one, as if making sure that's all they were. The coldness of it, and the rough hard texture, was reassuring.

She turned on her heel. Now where was the bloody house?

Carrying along up the path, she veered to the right, wondering what other statutes might inhabit the gardens here. Grecian gods and goddesses?

Finally, she saw it, looming in front of her. How could it ever have hidden itself so well? It was indeed huge. Not…Downton Abbey huge, but a pile, as she'd previously thought of it, something old, something…crumbling. Was that it? No way she could really tell that, not in such gloom. A house that had to date back to the Victorian era, or beyond even? Georgian, perhaps. Whatever. To her mind, it was ancient, and it gave the sense of something ancient. Wide-fronted, the main entrance more to the left than the middle, it had a deep pitched roof, and three tall chimneys. Ivy grew there as well, covering – or strangling – much of it. A house that *embraced* the darkness, no lights on anywhere that she could see.

*Jessica Lockhart, you must be loaded!*

It certainly knocked the house where she grew up – a 1950s suburban semi – out of the ballpark. That house, though, had been filled to the rafters, with parents, siblings, other family members and friends. No matter how small it was, all of them had crammed in there. This house was colossal. And yet just one person occupied it.

Jessica Lockhart, housebound but apparently not disabled, was at home there somewhere. In a rear room, perhaps?

She had to be.

Sniffing hard again, pulling her jacket even tighter, Isla ventured towards the front door. The key safe, the agency had told her, was to the right of the door. The code, 0101, wasn't the most secure in the world when she thought about it, not out here in the boondocks. Perhaps she should offer to change it to something less obvious. Funny how such emptiness could make you feel so vulnerable. Truth was, she was safer out here than in any town. There was no need to let city paranoia swamp her.

Just to the right… So where was it? She couldn't see it. Her hands patted at the wall, searching. Maybe the agency had got it wrong – it wouldn't be the first time – and it was to the left. She sidestepped the door, repeated the same actions, shaking her head in further frustration. There was no key safe anywhere.

"For God's sake…" There'd be a doorbell instead. She'd ring that. No ordinary doorbell, but an iron ring pull. Isla's expression caught between annoyance and amusement as she pulled at it.

She could hear the resultant ring from inside; more a creak than a ring, if she were honest. No light came on in response. There was no sound of movement, no shuffling of slippers that she expected. Maybe the woman was more disabled than she'd been told. Not a wheelchair user, but not able to walk without support.

But she had to at least try. Jessica needed Isla to assist her, and Isla needed to get inside the house, where she could dry off, charge her phone and call for help.

Intending to bang on the door, pummel it if necessary, she had a thought. This was the countryside, *deep* countryside, and what did people do around here, that she'd been told they did, over and over? They didn't lock their doors, that's what. *Because it's safe,* she reminded herself. *So safe.*

Her hand grabbing the doorknob, cold, bronze, and no doubt heavily tarnished, she pushed. She could have cried with relief when the door gave way.

With a triumphant shove, she pushed it further open and hurried inside. Her overriding feeling now was curiosity at what lay before her. It was a hallway, a *grand* hallway – most likely her entire flat would fit in it – but it was swamped in as much darkness as the outside. And as cold. Shivering, she wrapped her arms tight around herself. Why wasn't the heating on? The previous carer, the one who'd left in such a hurry, had they turned it off or something? She'd look into that as soon as possible. The cold was unpleasant enough for her, but for the elderly, it could be lethal.

First, though, she craved some light, searching either side of the door to find some switches. The sound of her boots was hollow on the wooden flooring. She flattened her hand against the wall, finding it as cold and as unforgiving as the urns.

"Where are they?" she muttered. "They must be here somewhere."

It was so silent inside. *A mausoleum.* A thought that caused further unease.

An impressive house, a house that most would covet, and yet there was no welcome here. Indeed, she felt most *un*welcome. As though a thousand pairs of eyes stared at her from the shadows, and all with scorn and derision.

"For Christ's sake, where are the fucking light switches?"

Her hand brushed against something other than the wall. Something smooth: a panel, either silver or brass, with three switches in a row. She flicked them all.

Light. At last. Swallowing the dark. Not a bright light, though, but muted; the shadows were still there, pooling in the corners.

Looking around, she saw a chandelier that hung in the middle of the ceiling and several wall sconces, all with a yellowish cast, initially flickering before settling.

There was furniture too: a few items, pushed close to the walls, a bench where you could sit and untie your footwear, a long narrow wooden table (the kind you might place a vase on), and a coat and hat stand, also empty.

The staircase was centrally positioned, darkness persisting at the top of it. Returning to the door, she shut it, and then, still curious, walked over to where there were two framed portraits – the only other decoration – by the side of the staircase.

One featured a young girl, around eight or nine Isla guessed, the other a boy who was younger still. They were romantic pieces; the kind Isla imagined an Old Master might produce. The girl, fair-haired, wearing a white smock and with pale pink ribbons in her hair, stood in front of a ruined rose-covered arch. The boy, who had dark hair, wore a pair of dark trousers and a white flouncy shirt, and sat in a high-backed armchair. His gaze was not as solemn as the girl's; a slight smile on his face hinted at mischievousness.

Neither sharp nor defined, they had instead a misty quality to them, their complexions as dewy as their eyes. Beautiful paintings, beautiful subjects. Who were they? Isla wondered. Those that had lived there before? If so, when? She found it impossible to date the portraits, to decide whether they were genuinely old or simply trying to capture the idealism of a bygone age. Suddenly, and overwhelmingly, she wanted to reach out, to touch the children, her fingers tracing the thick brushstrokes that had created them. *Who are you?* she questioned again. *What's your story?*

From being in an almost dreamlike state too, she frowned.

Was that laughter she heard?

A short burst of it.

Not from nearby, though. More distant than that,

muffled and therefore secretive.

Her frown deepened. Jessica Lockhart was supposed to live alone here. Was she responsible? It was such a light sound, though, the kind a child might make.

"Hello," she called out. "Jessica?"

Silence again, saturating everything. There'd been no laughter. Just like she'd imagined all those pairs of eyes on her, and the three cloaked figures outside, she'd imagined that. *You're bringing the house to life.* Crazy thoughts. *Tired* thoughts. What she needed to do was find the real occupant of this house, and make sure she was all right.

Removing her hat, gloves, rucksack and coat, she placed them all to the side, to sit in a puddle, and then called out again. "Jessica? Jessica Lockhart? It's Isla Barrow from the agency. Sorry I'm so late, I had a slight...um...accident on the way here. Jessica, where are you? I'm coming to find you, okay?"

No other lights were on as far as she could tell downstairs, and so she headed to the staircase.

"Jessica," she kept calling as she climbed, emerging onto the landing, desperate to find the light switch there as well. When she did, it illuminated a long narrow corridor that ran both in front and behind her, and several rooms with closed doors.

Dread seized her in the enduring silence. What if something had happened to Jessica – something...terrible? Yes, she'd been waylaid, but, overall, it hadn't been too big a gap between one carer leaving and the other showing up. No way that during that time Jessica could have...died.

Could she?

She had to find her, and fast. And if something terrible had happened, call an ambulance from the landline. Hope

22

they responded quickly. No way she wanted to wait too long in what was indeed a mausoleum, with only a cadaver for company.

A clap of thunder that made the windowpanes rattle in their frames caused her to yelp. So there was a storm outside now? The night was getting worse.

"Jessica? Jessica?"

She began running, trying the handle of the doors closest to her.

"JESSICA!"

Isla flung another door open. So many bedrooms, so much frenzy in her actions, the dust that she'd imagined in spare rooms, flying upwards, equally agitated.

*Where the hell are you?*

Her heart was beating as wildly as before, the thunder still rolling, shaking not only the windows but the house itself. She barely caught a reply.

And when she did, it inspired both relief and further dread.

"Help!"

# Chapter Three

## 21ˢᵗ/22ⁿᵈ December

A woman in her eighties, Rog Ditton had said, but the woman Isla encountered seemed far older than that, as ancient as the house she lived in.

Following the woman's voice as she cried for help, Isla burst into another bedroom. This one had a magnificent bed, a four-poster, intricately carved. But that was as far as the romanticism she'd also encountered downstairs went. There were bare floorboards beneath her feet, not even a rug to cover them to lend some comfort. A dressing table, but the mirror was clouded, and what lay on the surface of it – a comb, a brush, a hand mirror, and what looked like some dried-up cosmetics – all strewn haphazardly across it. Not bare walls – there was wallpaper, a flocked pattern in cream and gold – but it was dark in the corners, and it was mouldy, some edges having peeled away. At the windows there were curtains, but she got the impression that if she drew them apart once morning came, they'd turn to dust.

And the air stank of human effluence. Jessica, who was lying half on the bed and half off it, had soiled herself.

"Oh my God, Jessica, Ms Lockhart, I'm here, I'm coming. So sorry for being late. But I'm here now. Oh…God."

Like a bird, that's what she reminded Isla of. Whose wings were thrashing.

"What's happened?" the woman replied, her voice shrill. "Look what's happened! No use. Any of it. I've waited. So long. Is it you? Are you there? Show yourself!"

"I'm sorry, really really sorry. Come on, let me help you."

Isla rushed over and tried to lift the woman back on to the bed, but ended up half-dragging her. The woman protested. Arms as thin as twigs continued to flail and clutch at the air, but somehow Isla got her on there, then rolled her onto her side to quickly release the dirty sheet from beneath her.

When the woman was quiet at last, her voice having dissolved into murmurings, Isla grabbed the dirty linen and rushed out of the room with it, hoping to find a bathroom. This was most likely the master suite, if Jessica was occupying it, and so the bathroom had to be close by, hopefully next door.

That's where she ran, releasing one hand to open the door, cursing when it resisted her and wondering why it should. This was a room that was used often, surely? But still it fought against her, until she barged at it with the side of her body, wincing because the impact made the injuries she'd sustained in the car crash hurt more. She was successful, though, and it opened at last. A bathroom, yes, but not one that contained anything modern. It had one of those huge tubs, with a roll top and clawed feet, and thick crusts of limescale where the tap had drip, drip, dripped.

She threw the linen in the bath and then struggled next with the taps, trying to turn them, a clank that could compete with the thunder as finally they relented. Whilst the bath filled – slowly, reluctantly – she turned to the sink, huffing and puffing, and staring at her reflection in the mottled mirror above it.

Twenty-four, that's how old she was, but there was no spark of youth about her, not any more. Nothing to light up the green of her eyes. Her dark hair was plastered to her skull from the hat she'd worn, lifeless and stringy when once she'd fussed over it. She used to wear plenty of eyeliner and mascara too. She tried to smile at the Isla that used to be, but tears blurred her vision further. Like the landscape she was in, she'd been wild too, once upon a time. Eager to live life, to seize it with both hands. But isn't that what the young were supposed to do? Why worry about the future so much, about what time carved you into, a husk, like that woman in the other room, lying in her own mess, alone and lonely?

*It's not all about you, Isla!*

That's what she'd been told, over and over.

And she hadn't listened.

"It's not all about you…"

She murmured those same words, as drenched as her, but in pain and sorrow.

Pushing away from the sink, she turned back to the bath, her wet clothes cold and sticky, but nothing she could do about that for the moment. Water from the tap was still trying to wash away the worst of the filth, or maybe it was a thankless task and she should just throw the sheets away and find new ones. Doubts were already forming as to whether there was a washing machine here, or any nod to mod cons.

With a sigh, she crossed over to a tall cupboard by the side of the bath, yanked it open, and rummaged around in there looking for items she could use. There was a bowl for some warm water, the stub of a soap, although it was ingrained with dirt, and some flannels and towels. Not a great selection; just a few of them, and each as threadbare as everything else she'd discovered so far, as the blinds at the bathroom window, which she daren't pull to shut the weather out, the jagged lightning flashing.

With everything to hand, she went back into the bedroom. The woman was still murmuring, seemingly lost in a world of her own.

Getting to work, she noticed the bare mattress was stained, perhaps from previous accidents. Also, on a bedside table, there was no medication to hand. There should be tablets for blood pressure and cholesterol, so she'd have to search them out and make sure that Jessica took her usual dose. The only things on the table were a lamp, an empty water glass and a pair of spectacles, one arm of which was held on by tape. No books, no magazines, nothing that could keep a person entertained. She'd call Rog Ditton when her phone was charged, but maybe not tonight. She'd do it first thing in the morning. It would be far easier to sort everything out then, and she'd ask again why the previous carer had quit. *Carer?* No matter how cantankerous Jessica was, whoever had abandoned her in this state was no carer.

"Jessica," she said, "where do you keep fresh bedding?"

"What?" Jessica replied, her eyes closing. "Who?"

Shaking her head, Isla began to rummage again, through drawers in the bedroom, in search of medication and linen, and also a mobile phone, just in case Jessica might have one tucked away somewhere. No sign of medication or a phone, but linen was there at least, in amongst a heap of clothes and underwear that reeked of mothballs. Everything in the room, Jessica included, felt as though it would crumble to dust easily. *Crumbling lives,* she thought with such sadness.

*You and me both.*

At last the bed had, if not fresh, fresh*er* sheets on it, and Jessica had been washed and changed into a long white nightdress. Tucking her up, Isla tiptoed from the room, thinking her asleep already.

She was wrong, though. Just before she closed the door, she heard the woman murmur again, a repeat of the first word she'd ever heard from her lips.

"Help."

* * *

What a night it had been! What a predicament she was in!

Morning had at last arrived, even though at one point Isla was sure it never would, the gloom that lingered at Wildacre permanent. The weather hadn't improved through the night. Rain was continuing to lash at the windows, the glass panes as fragile as their host, and Isla feared they'd cave under the pressure and just…explode. Even today, whilst she stood in the kitchen staring out of the window, it hadn't really improved. No more thunder and lightning, but the rain was heavy still. She'd get drenched going to her car, as soaked as she'd been last night. Her chest was sore this morning, and a cough tickled at her throat. The back of her head where she'd hit it was aching, and her neck too – probably the result of whiplash.

But go she must. At some point. Because she'd been stupid, a real idiot.

Her mobile was dead, and she'd forgotten her charger. And, so far, she hadn't found a landline at Wildacre either. The previous night, still in wet clothes, she'd had a quick look around but no luck. What she *had* found, however, was still troubling her, the way that the house was. Before coming down to the kitchen, she'd been in briefly to check on Jessica, who'd been awake but mumbling. She'd asked her about a landline, but no luck there either. The woman just carried on mumbling.

She needed her mobile, that was the long and short of it. She'd been *sure* she'd packed the charger. But when she'd looked, after choosing the bedroom closest to Jessica and emptying the contents of her rucksack, she couldn't find it.

Stranded. That's what she felt like. And in all places, this.

"Shit! Shit! Shit!" she swore, feeling absolutely wretched. "And now you've caught a cold for your troubles. You might even infect Jessica and finish her off."

How had the previous carer coped?

"Carer, my arse," she spat. Isla sincerely hoped that whoever it was would be sacked, especially after she told Rog about the state Jessica was in on her arrival.

Her nostrils flared. No, they wouldn't be sacked. Carers were thin on the ground, two reasons being long hours and crap pay. They'd better hope, though, that they didn't cross paths when Isla was back in Alnwick. She wouldn't go easy on them.

Turning her back on the window and the grim outside, she again surveyed the grim inside. The kitchen, like everywhere else she'd seen so far, was covered in dust and cobwebs. There was some food, but nothing fresh; just rows of tins in the cupboards, most of them looking well past their sell-by date. She also had to find some way of getting groceries, some milk for tea and cereal, bread, butter, that kind of thing. Again, she was cross with the previous carer. Isla might be considered selfish, but whoever had been in charge of Jessica was tarred with the same brush.

No use standing there, complaining. She had a job to do. Galvanising herself, she went over to the kettle, grabbed it and filled it with water, rolling her eyes when the implement wheezed rather than burst into life. At least there were teabags in a ceramic jar. She took one out, sniffed it, rolled her eyes like she'd done before, then found a couple of mugs that had to be thoroughly scrubbed before being filled. The heating was on. She'd cranked it into life, but the water remained cold. The system was just too old to have much of an impact.

Breakfast would have to be tinned fruit. Peaches and prunes. Not too much of the latter for Jessica, though. Isla didn't want a repeat incident of the previous night. She supposed they wouldn't starve, as she took the tins down, an outbreak of coughing ensuing. *This'll turn into pneumonia if I'm not careful,* the wry thought running through her head. *I'll be housebound too, stuck in bed.*

The bed… Oh God, the room she'd slept in! Only now it was sinking in what she was having to endure. What Jessica had endured – and in her case, for how long?

Isla had no idea where that other carer had rested their head, but it wasn't in the room she'd chosen. That was a room that had lain undisturbed, as barren as Jessica's, with only the essentials in it: a bed, a wardrobe, a bedside table and a lamp. That was it. Nothing more. No paintings adorning the walls, or in any other room she'd been in – only the two in the hallway, and those in pride of place. She hadn't yet counted how many bedrooms there were at Wildacre, but there had to be at least six or seven. Were all of them similar to hers, and Jessica's too? Any homely touches…gone.

There'd been sheets on the bed in her room at least, and

a coverlet, but again Isla had felt that sense of decay when she'd touched them. The dust that had risen when she'd pulled at them had set off the coughing, and she hadn't really stopped since, too much of it ingested she supposed. Remembering thinking there might be housework here, plenty to keep her occupied, she could have laughed. It wasn't just a case of dusting and polishing; the house needed gutting. Impressive it may be, in terms of size, but it was stuck in the past, with everything – *everything* – left to rot.

As she opened the tinned fruit, the smell of it sickly sweet, she tried to temper her thoughts. Her bed was old, dusty, it smelt of mothballs and old age, and yet it was serviceable, just. She'd tried not to notice the mould and cobwebs that had gathered in the corners, eventually sleeping, and sleeping well. She'd dreamed, but the dreams had been muddled: images, random at best, filling her head, sliding in, then sliding out. And in her dreams she was sure she'd heard laughter again, echoing down the corridors – but strangely, she hadn't minded it; she'd almost welcomed it. Laughter was something very much needed at Wildacre.

Looking at the tinned fruit in a bowl – just for Jessica, as she'd decided against having any herself, the sight of such pallid lumps congealing in front of her destroying any hunger she might have felt – Isla tried to recall more of her wayward dreams. Laughter and…footsteps? Was that it? A heavy tread, though; not light or fleeting, the kind that Jessica would be responsible for. She might even have called out as she'd done on the approach to the house, 'Who are you?'

As she now tried to find a tray to place the bowl and a mug of tea on – pray God, Jessica wouldn't have a fit when she saw the tea had no milk – a frown was back on her face.

There was something a bit off about the dreams she'd had, actually, that had…agitated her a little. Had she called out, as she thought, or was it another voice she'd heard? One with…anger in it? Malice, even? Ah, who knew? She didn't usually pay too much attention to dreams. She knew what nonsense they could be.

With the tray in her hands, she glanced out of the window a final time before leaving the kitchen. Surely the rain would ease soon? If it did, that's when she'd make a dash for it and head down the road to her car. The charger may have fallen out of her rucksack when she was rummaging, not just for her mobile but later her hat and gloves, and in her shock she hadn't noticed. She hadn't thought to check the weather report before coming here, and now, of course, couldn't. It rained a lot up north, she knew that much, the sky so much darker in winter, a cold that had jaws.

She returned to the hallway, there to climb the stairs, the tray balanced in her hands, careful not to spill anything. Those portraits… She'd have to ask Jessica about them, who they were, and hope she'd get an intelligible answer.

Up and up she climbed, to the landing, where the runner beneath her feet was supposed to be red but had long since faded to pink, and was fraying at the edges. So worn, all of it, but in the right hands it could be restored. No doubt it'd be sold after Jessica died; some long-lost family member coming out of the woodwork to lay claim, rubbing their hands together in glee at the prospect of owning it – a project, for sure, but there may be some profit in it. Shame they couldn't earn what was coming to them by seeing to their benefactress whilst she was alive and clearly in need, but no, others would do that – those that got paid for it, even if it was a pittance.

"She's not dead yet, Isla," she told herself on reaching her bedroom door.

Having previously left it ajar, she pushed at it with the side of her arm.

"Jessica," she called out brightly. "As promised, I've brought you breakfast."

To her surprise, Jessica wasn't lying down murmuring, but sitting upright.

"Hey there!" Isla continued. "Glad to see you're more awake now."

In the room's gloom, the old woman turned to her, her expression…glazed. They were as good as strangers, admitted, but Isla had expected at least some form of recognition. But it was as if the woman was staring at a distant point beyond her.

Without saying another word, Isla made room for the tray on the dressing table. She then went over to the curtains and pulled them apart. *Let there be light,* the words running through her mind while she did so. It was barely an improvement.

As she'd done in the kitchen below, she gazed out, albeit briefly, and thought she spied something through the trees. Was it…? Could it be…? Headstones? Two of them, hard, cold, grey things, poking up through the grass. She shivered. Was there a graveyard in the grounds of Wildacre? She guessed some big houses might have them, family plots. Is that what it was, a space left for Jessica too? She exhaled as she shook her head. What a place this was! A strange, strange place. And what a strange Christmas it was going to be. Perhaps, even, the Christmas she deserved.

She swung around. Jessica was still staring in the same

direction. At what?

High blood pressure and high cholesterol were all Jessica Lockhart was supposed to suffer from. Isla walked back to the dressing table with the tray on. When she brought it over, the woman suddenly lifted her hand and knocked the tray. As the contents of the bowl and mug spilled everywhere, as Isla yelped as hot liquid just missed her, she had to wonder if Rog hadn't been quite truthful when seeking emergency cover for this woman. In order to get Isla out there, at such short notice, a few days before Christmas, he'd left out one very important detail.

That she also had dementia.

# Chapter Four

## 22<sup>nd</sup> December

The tea thankfully hadn't scalded either Isla or Jessica, but the bedding had to be partially changed, Isla's charge sitting mute whilst she did so. Outbursts, that's what she was prone to, like a lot of patients with dementia or Alzheimer's. Not that Isla was skilled in dealing with them; she wasn't. Of the clients she saw to, some did indeed suffer from such an illness, but only the very early stages. Jessica's condition was clearly advanced. No way Isla could be angry with her for what she'd done. It could be that Jessica forgot about her as soon as she left the room, falling back into a world of her own making. Subsequently, Isla's 'sudden' appearance would be so frightening, so confusing, that no wonder she'd react adversely to it. Isla would just have to work out how to deal with the situation. Tread more carefully. Unlike the other carer, she wouldn't walk out on her. Getting to the main road, though, waiting to flag someone down, could take hours. Could she leave her alone for that long? She might do worse than soil herself. She might fall out of bed and break her bones.

"I'll tell you what," Isla said, once she'd finished clearing up the mess, "I'll get you another drink and some more fruit. I'm sorry but there doesn't seem to be any fresh food in the house, only tinned, but I'll sort that out too." *Somehow.*

"No! Don't!"

Startled by her sudden coherence, Isla inclined her head. "Sorry... I—"

Jessica's eyes were decidedly more focused now, darting from side to side, as if scanning the room for something. Something...fearful?

"It's okay," Isla tried to soothe. "I'm here. Don't worry."

"Don't want...eat," Jessica croaked.

"You have to. I know it's not much, but—"

"DON'T EAT!"

Isla conceded. "Okay, all right. You don't have to eat, not just yet. Would you..." she searched for a chair that she could pull forwards, and spied one in a near corner, one she'd need to brush mildew from, "...like me to sit with you instead?"

Jessica said neither yes nor no, and so Isla brought the chair over anyway, dusted it down as best she could, then sat. *Silently* sat. As did Jessica. A shell of a woman. She really was so frail, skeletal almost. When was the last time she'd eaten a proper meal? She was...wasting away. For the umpteenth time, anger at the previous carer flared. You didn't walk out on a client just because they were difficult.

The depth of outrage she felt on Jessica's behalf surprised her. Where was it coming from? Isla, who simply did her job and never got attached. Didn't *deserve* attachment of any kind, not any more. She was selfish, through and through, and yet here she was, suddenly flooded with compassion?

"Jessica," she said, her voice softer than ever, "how long have you lived here?"

When the woman continued to stare, Isla dared to reach out and touch her, fingertips brushing papery skin on the back of the woman's hand. It had the effect she hoped for. Jessica shook her head slightly, focusing on Isla rather than something fictional in the corner of the room. The shadows that were there.

"Lived here?" she said.

"Yes," Isla replied. "A fair while, I should imagine."

Again, the woman repeated what she'd said. "A fair while? I… Yes. Yes!"

Scratching for something else to say, Isla continued. "It's a beautiful house. Remote, though. Do you…um…get many visitors?"

"Yes."

"Really? People come and see you often?"

"Yes," Jessica mouthed.

Hard work talking to her. Getting her nowhere fast. And the information she was getting, she wasn't buying it. This house *screamed* of loneliness. As Isla was about to ask who it was that visited – family, friends, or both – Jessica's gaze strayed elsewhere in the room, one hand lifting to clutch at the neck of her nightdress.

"Jessica?" Isla said, unable to stop herself from rising and staring around the room too. Fictional shadows, she'd called them earlier, but actually, on closer inspection, gloom *had* cast shapes there, each one varying in depth. Even so, she sought to assure her client. "There's no one there. Nothing to see. Look, are you sure you don't want to eat? If not fruit, I'll find something else. Water. I'll fetch some water." She'd put some by her bed before she'd left last night, but it remained untouched. "That'd be nice, wouldn't it? Cool, clean water? You must be parched."

Viper-quick, the woman turned her head towards Isla. "Clean? You think anything here is clean?"

"Yes… No… Look, we can change all that. I'll do some housework—"

"Shoo! Shoo! Go on! Get out! I don't want you here. I don't want…anyone." Her voice cracked as she said that, as if she were saying the words but didn't believe them. As if she was *desperate* for someone. "Too late," she continued, rambling again. "Everything's changed. Everything's different. I am. Look at me. Look at me!"

A clear case of dementia. And here was Isla, a novice, having to deal with it. Trapped. In a nightmare. She'd thought that before, when she'd crashed the car, when she'd had to get out and walk, what a nightmare it was, but now it had gone from bad to worse. *If only I hadn't forgotten the charger!*

"So…different now…you've changed too! You there? Are! Are!"

Jessica was railing, but not at Isla any more – her eyes were back on the shadows. Shadows that…writhed in protest? That moved?

*For fuck's sake, Isla! Of course they're not moving.*

She had to calm her, but how?

"Jessica, please! It's okay, it's all right. There's no one there, in the corners."

It worked this time, what she'd said.

Jessica stopped abruptly. Also just as suddenly, she lay down, but still clutching her gown, her fingers working hard against the soft cotton material. And there were words on her lips, mere whisperings. The word '*Help*' amongst them?

Isla tried to listen, to catch at least something of what was being said, but failed. If she drew nearer, perhaps she'd have more luck. But she couldn't bring herself to do it, hoping, praying, now *begging* a deity – one she ordinarily had no contact with, had never quite believed in, especially in recent times – that the woman would sleep, just sleep. That's what the elderly did, didn't they? Slept. One foot in the grave already.

It seemed Jessica was indeed drifting. Isla sighed with relief. Good. Long may it last. Could she do it, whilst her client was sleeping? Make a break for it and head back to the car to check it over for the charger? If the God she was suddenly calling on for help was really good to her, she'd pass another car on the way, someone else also having cause to travel down this dirt track, and she could flag them down.

Help… They were both in such dire need.

Around two to three miles to the car, and the same distance back. A couple of hours walking. Less if she really hurried, if she practically ran all the way.

Isla's chest heaved, and she coughed. An ear-splitting, hacking sound.

No way she could run. Her energy was every bit as drained as the battery on her phone. She was loath to leave Jessica for that long and not be on hand, but something had to be done about this situation. Stealing from the room, as she'd done several times already in the short space of time she'd been there, she'd go now and return to the house as quickly as possible, the house of shadows…

As she entered the corridor, once again she had that feeling of being watched.

\* \* \*

A futile journey. And she was cold, wet through again, coughing and coughing, her chest feeling like someone was stamping on it with heavy boots.

There'd been no charger in the car. She'd searched, she'd sworn, even screamed at one point. *YOU HAVE GOT TO BE KIDDING!* Of all things to forget, why did it have to be that? Why not something inconsequential? Her toothbrush, for example, something she could live without. Likely, the charger was at home still, in the socket by her bedside, of no use to anyone. Tears of utter frustration filled her eyes. Even worse, there was no traffic. No chance of flagging anyone down.

She could walk to the main road from her car. *Not* a main road, she reminded herself, another bloody country road – but it was at least better than this track she'd found herself on. It was a mile or so more, though, and then there was the return journey to consider if no car passed, and the fatigue she was feeling. Could she leave Jessica alone for much longer? What would be the lesser of two evils?

Isla didn't know, couldn't think. So cold, and yet she felt as though she was burning. The chill she'd caught really taking hold.

*What about the other way?* Maybe there was a house closer to Wildacre but in the opposite direction. It was perfectly possible.

She could go back to the house, dry off, tend to Jessica, maybe even grab an hour's rest, then trudge up the road the other way.

A better plan. It made more sense. Everything just too far in the other direction.

After checking the car one last time, underneath and all around it, praying the charger would just suddenly appear, she headed back, trying to keep the lid on the anger she felt at her own behaviour – *again*. Self-hatred was a terrible thing. As young as she was, she knew that – and yet there it was, laying down roots.

The pillars came into view. Walking up to them, she tore at some of the ivy with stiffened fingers. Was there a plaque there, but hidden? How hard her fingers worked to untangle it, but sure enough, there *were* words carved into the pillar, *Wildacre*, although lichen also did its best to obscure them, having sunk into the grooves. *So damned secretive,* she thought, *this house that hides from the world.*

As she continued past the pillars, the rain eased, although the sky remained as threatening, the grey of it like pewter. *Merry bloody Christmas,* she thought, heading up the gravel driveway. A driveway as impressive as the house, she could see that now. It was long and wide, and the trees either side resplendent, a mix of several species, chestnuts and oaks. She could veer off the path that curved around to the house, and head towards the back of it instead, drawn by something she'd seen there only this morning from the window of Jessica's bedroom.

The headstones, of course. She wanted to know who was buried there, and when.

There was an urgency in her step which she marvelled at, how *much* she wanted to know. This, despite feeling so unwell, so tired, and despite Jessica too.

*Just a few more minutes, that's all I'll be.*

The grass had grown so tall round there, and the grounds were every bit as unkempt as the house. She waded through it, glad that she had worn leather boots instead of her usual Converse – the canvas would be ruined by now if she had. On reaching the headstones, she crouched and read what was engraved there, brushing at the lichen obscuring some of it. *Amelia 1953-1960* was inscribed on one, and *Gabriel, 1955-1960* on the other. *Amelia and Gabriel, Amelia and*

*Gabriel…* There was also an epitaph, the same on each, but it was the names and dates that revolved in her head, the girl seven when she'd died and the boy five. Were these the children depicted in the portraits in the hallway? Vividly, she recalled them. The girl in her white smock, with the archway behind her, roses on the arch, pink, of course, to match the ribbons in her hair. Such a pretty girl, her hair gleaming, her eyes blue – a *misty* blue, due to the ethereal nature of the painting. The boy in his dark trousers and white shirt was also the epitome of sweet innocence.

She wondered why there wasn't also a portrait of Jessica in the hallway, or anywhere in the house she'd been so far – although, she admitted, she'd conducted only a whirlwind tour so far. There could even be a family portrait somewhere, of the children, Jessica, and their father. Perhaps…Jessica had had the paintings done posthumously? Both children had died in the same year: 1960. Why? What had been the cause? Jessica Lockhart had carried on, into the arms of old age, and amnesia. Not an illness, but something forced because of tragedy?

Oh, what did Isla know about any of it? Nothing.

Only that she felt sorrier for Jessica than ever. *You're a lost soul.*

To the side of the graves there was something else, something that caused Isla to screw up her face in further confusion. A mound, covered in ivy and weeds.

Curious and curiouser. Another grave – it must be – but this one unmarked.

# Chapter Five

## *22<sup>nd</sup> December*

"Where are you? Are you there? Tell me, are you?"

As soon as she entered the house, Isla could hear Jessica shouting. Damn it. She'd been gone too long after all.

As she raced up the stairs, taking them two at a time, all kinds of scenarios played in her head: Jessica lying in her own filth again, or she'd tumbled out of bed and fallen to the floor breaking an arm or a leg, or both. What the hell would Isla do then? Leave her in agony as she bolted back out of the house, going in the opposite direction to before as she'd previously decided, willing another house to be within striking distance, to just…materialise? This county – it really was as it boasted: sparse. Never had she felt so alone! So helpless!

Isla burst into Jessica's bedroom, coughing from all the recent exertion, her eyes half-closed as she winced, hardly daring to see what was in front of her.

Jessica was out of bed, but not fallen. She'd made her way over to the window and was clinging to the sill, her back hunched.

"Oh, Jessica! What are you doing? If you want to get out of bed, you should have waited for me. I'd have helped you."

Thankfully, she hadn't soiled herself. One thing less to

deal with.

Having reached her, Isla cajoled her further. "Let me get you back into bed."

"No. Not bed!"

"Jessica, I need to get you into bed, where you're safe."

"Safe?"

Isla changed tack. "Are you hurt? Does anywhere feel sore?"

"I want… I want… Out."

Isla was truly perplexed. Where did she think she could go? "Jessica, honestly, you must come back to bed. We can go somewhere else later, downstairs, perhaps. Come on, that's it, take my arm. You are safe. You're with me."

Incredibly, the woman complied, one hand gripping Isla as she placed her arm around Jessica's waist, half carrying her to the four-poster.

"Oh, Jessica," Isla whispered as she steered her onwards. She was skin and bone, nothing more. She had to get her to eat today, and if not eat, at least drink something. *You poor, poor thing.*

"No use," Jessica was mumbling as she took a series of tiny steps. "No use, no use, no use. Blame me. Not just me! My fault. Sorry. Sorry. Sorry."

Having reached the bed, Isla sitting Jessica down on it, the old woman crumpled, her body folding in on itself as the tears came, her shoulders heaving.

Isla steeled herself as she drew the woman closer, stunned again when Jessica allowed it.

"I'm sorry," Isla said, echoing Jessica, although in that moment, she didn't know what for exactly – only that she meant it, and that tears were forming in her own eyes. It was just so hard to see someone this distressed, sobs and wails ringing out, despair tipping from one heart and into the other. *The last thing I need is more despair!* She'd run from that, from reactions to actions, and yet now here she was, having to face a similar depth of emotion, but with a stranger.

The sobbing at last quietened as Jessica tried to form words. Was she saying something about orphans? Isla drew back slightly so she could hear.

"Orphans. Caught…storm. Eternal…storm."

Orphans? Who was she referring to? Amelia and Gabriel? She'd adopted them?

"Jessica, if you get into bed, I can get you a drink, something warm and soothing. Please let me help you. That's what I'm here for."

Slowly, painfully, Jessica lifted her head.

"You're here…for that?"

Isla nodded enthusiastically. "Yes! To take care of you. You're not alone."

"Not…alone."

"Not any more. I know…I know things haven't been easy, that you *have* been alone. And recently, I had to go out, to my car, further down the lane. I crashed it on the way here, last night. It's not a serious crash. I'm not hurt or anything. Well, a bit bruised, but otherwise I'm okay. I needed a charger for my mobile and I thought it might be in the car. There doesn't seem to be a working phone here, unless…unless you know differently? Then…well, then we could call someone, to deliver groceries, to get my car fixed." *An ambulance at this rate,* she thought, but didn't say it, more fear rising in her. Jessica Lockhart was very old, very frail, very confused, and wouldn't eat or drink. Was she actually closer to death than to life? Could it be imminent?

If so, it would be harder still for Isla to leave her. After she'd passed…well, then there'd be all the time in the world. She could walk all day to find help. Her task now, perhaps, was to make Jessica's end more bearable. *Make amends.*

Unable to stop herself, Isla reached out again to hug the woman. Not a bad woman, and perhaps every right to be cantankerous. From what she was saying, Jessica Lockhart was someone who'd adopted children and formed a family, only to lose them both in the same year, the same month, maybe even the same day.

The woman was stiff in her arms this time. She seemed…surprised by what Isla was doing. As well she might. Appalled even?

Isla released her, was all business-like again. *That's what this arrangement is,* she reminded herself, *a business situation. Nothing more.*

"Right, come on, let's get you into bed." She adopted her best no-nonsense voice, the one she used with a lot of clients – God, she hated that word, *clients,* but it was the term the agency insisted you use. Thankfully, Jessica obeyed, swinging like a pendulum from protest to docility, hour by hour, minute by minute. She was spent, most likely. They both were. Emotionally and physically shattered.

"I'll…um…I'll get some tea, and some water. I need you to take a few sips, Jessica, that's all. It really will make you feel so much better."

As she backtracked towards the door, she questioned whether she could handle it when the time finally came. Dementia was one thing, but *death*? Better for it to happen during daylight hours than in the middle of the night. To go out there again, in the pitch black, in heavy wind and rain, *an eternal storm,* with the ghost of Jessica Lockhart in her head… *Please God, let it happen in daylight!*

Jessica was mumbling as she left the room. Isla caught fragments.

"I saw you…"

Isla swung around. "You saw me?" She was confused, and then realisation hit her. Jessica must have been standing by the window when Isla had been at the graves. "I'm…sorry for your loss. Your children."

"Orphans," Jessica replied.

"Were they? Amazing. It's such a wonderful thing to do––"

"The storm, *the tempest*…will it ever end?"

\* \* \*

Isla brought tea and water, but Jessica was asleep by the time she returned, bony fingers still clutching at her nightdress, her breath laboured. She'd heard about the death rattle, and so leaned closer to see if she could detect such a thing, a sound apart, but decided she couldn't. Relief flooded her.

As tempted as she was to leave the house right now and go in the opposite direction continuing her quest for help, the heavens had opened further. The rain was now worse than ever, a deluge. Downstairs, she'd had a coughing fit, and her chest and back ached even more because of it. She felt feverish, but her forehead and cheeks, for now, remained cool. Best not to push it, though, to have Jessica die, then herself laid up in bed unable to move due to the flu. She should be patient and see what transpired in the next day or so. They could exist on tinned goods, and even if Jessica refused to touch food, there was water and shelter at least.

Having returned to the kitchen, she wrinkled her nose at

the state of it. Dirty. The whole house was. Whoever had cared for Jessica in the past, the one that had abandoned her, and even others before them, clearly hadn't cared to take on extra duties. But she would. *For a dying woman, Isla? What's the point?* She knew what the point was: to keep herself occupied, busy, busy, busy, so she wouldn't have to think. Selfish reasons, but she rolled up her sleeves nonetheless.

Hours passed. There were very few cleaning products in the kitchen – just a bottle of *Jif* whose contents had largely dried up, circa the last century she'd bet. She did what she could, though: rearranged cupboards, sorted out what edible food there was, even ate some of it – a beef stew that she tried not to look too closely at, lumps of meat more grey than brown, white globules of fat suspended in the jelly-like gravy. *Needs must when the devil drives.* That was one of her mum's favourite sayings. She used to utter that about every type of situation. But her mum, her own family, weren't her focus, not when Jessica's family intrigued her so much.

With surfaces wiped, the empty fridge given a wipe around too, and the floor mopped, all with cold water and nothing else, she stood back to assess her efforts. Not exactly gleaming, but it'd do, even if the smell of age lingered. Where next?

Maybe now she should explore the rest of the house more fully. She'd only really peeked into rooms, trying to find a telephone rather than for any other reason. What she'd found hadn't exactly tempted her to do more. It had disturbed her, if she was honest. But in the absence of anything else to do, it was again needs must.

From the kitchen, she entered the hallway, then ventured down the corridor to the far side of the house. There were three rooms to choose from, all with doors shut.

Picking a room, she reached out and turned the handle – brass handles, just as there were upstairs – knowing what she'd find inside from her brief foray before. A living room – at least that's what she suspected it was. Hard to tell when sheets covered everything, when cobwebs hung from corners, more dirt, and more mould – no one had *lived* in this room for years. Previously, her eyes had scanned the walls looking for a phone point, but now she wondered about those sheets, and whether she should tear them off, liberating what was beneath them. Sheets that reminded her of ghosts. Or maybe it was the house that was a ghost, a shadow of itself.

Sighing, she closed her eyes. She could continue standing in the doorway, as she'd done before, or just get rid of those awful sheets. This had been a family home, not a mausoleum. Furniture was hiding beneath, not ghouls of any kind.

Before she could change her mind, she found the light switch, again cursing how weak the light was from the overhead bulbs. Venturing a few steps further, she felt sick to her stomach, butterflies within performing a *danse macabre.*

A house such as this was designed for life. It *still* had life in it, and yet it had also been shut down. Although not wholly abandoned, parts of it certainly were, life lived in miniature, if it had been lived at all. Sixty years ago Amelia and Gabriel had died, and therefore the amount of time that Jessica had lived like this?

The curtains were partially closed. She walked over to them and pulled them apart, the rain-splattered windows making a surrealist painting of what was outside. *Trapped.* Again, she thought it. Because she couldn't leave. Not yet.

*Trapped like Jessica, like those lying in the ground out there, in all this rain.*

Another coughing fit seized her, and this time she was glad of it, for it offered a distraction from the path her thoughts were leading her down. If only there was some medication in the cupboards, some paracetamol, a bit of cough mixture in a sticky bottle, anything would do, but, just as Jessica's medications were absent, so was anything that might help with this chill she'd caught. *What a shitshow!* she seethed.

A sound behind her offered another distraction. It was a…*scampering* of some sort. Not in the room, but outside it, in the corridor.

She swung around, one hand rubbing at her chest although her skin prickled all over. "Hello? Who is it? Is anyone there?"

Had it been the sound of footsteps, those that she'd dreamed of?

"There's no one here," she whispered. "Just you and Jessica."

So what was responsible, then? A rat? And if so, a *large* rat?

Again, she felt sick. Was she trapped here with them too? Along with spiders, were they the only other thing that flourished?

Her feet made the floorboards creak as she hurried towards the corridor, past furniture that remained covered. She saw nothing that could be held responsible for the noise: certainly no army of rats ganging up on her. Confused, she swallowed hard, and got on with the business of inspecting the other two rooms in this part of the house. One looked like a snug, and one a library; two of its walls were lined with a series of floor-to-ceiling shelves, although all were empty. As in the living room, main items of furniture were covered in sheets. She no longer hesitated; she tore the sheets off, her courage clearly building. Quality pieces of furniture lay beneath, not the shoddy stuff she was used to. Isla reckoned some pieces were antique, and therefore worth some money. She opened the curtains in the library too, flinching at sudden movement, and pushing it hastily from her to see a large spider in the folds.

"Hurry back to your web," she muttered. "And stay there."

The rooms on the other side of the house comprised another living room, a study, and a dining room, all containing furniture but nothing personal, as if anything personal – mementoes, photographs, that kind of thing – had been buried too.

Dismayed by the state of the rooms and the mountains of dust that had collected, Isla wondered again not about the point of cleaning anything, but the *possibility* of it. She glanced upwards, towards the ceiling. If Jessica wasn't going to last long, there really would be no point. And yet, as she'd already concluded, it at least gave *her* something to do. *So come on, Isla, pick a room, any room.*

She chose the main living room. There was a gorgeous fireplace in there, carved in black marble, and an empty grate within. It was perfectly possible that there might even be a wood store somewhere in the grounds. She could drag some logs in and get a fire going, then coax Jessica downstairs to sit in front of it for a while. Despite the heating turned up full, cold permeated everything. *Jessica's* room was cold. So to have some heat on her bones, she might welcome it. It could even perk her up a bit.

More plans coming together that she'd press into action.

First, though, she'd check on Jessica, then explore the bedrooms too.

# Chapter Six

## 22<sup>nd</sup> December

How long could a person sleep? *One foot in the grave, remember?* With that in mind, Isla supposed Jessica could sleep for a long, long time. Which was good, handy even, no need to complain about it. But as the only other living, breathing person in the house – for now at least – Isla found that she missed her. She *wanted* to hear her speak, even if it was garbled rubbish. All that stuff about orphans and storms sounded familiar. Wasn't there a saying along those lines? Another one she'd heard her mum say? *We're all orphans of the storm.* That was it. A strange saying, but then so many were. A lot of them were dying out: the younger generations weren't using them so much. New speak was coming in, a lot of text speech, a special kind of slang. So much was dying, really. Certainly her old way of life had, because of a mistake – *one* mistake, but which her family viewed as one of many.

*Don't think about that now! Or them. Explore!*

Incredibly, a smile played on her lips. Exploring here was like a game. Open the door and see what's inside…what would scamper by…jump out at you.

Just rats and spiders, nothing worse. It was a good job she wasn't phobic. Maybe that was why the last carer had left so suddenly: because a big spider had dropped on them from the ceiling above, and petrified, they'd legged it.

Isla nodded wryly. *Like I said, just not paid enough.*

If that had been the case, perhaps she could find sympathy for them after all.

Upstairs, there was Jessica's bedroom (which Isla knew well enough), the narrow old-fashioned bathroom beside it, and opposite that, the bedroom she'd chosen.

Her throat tickling, but trying not to cough and wake Jessica, she moved quietly up the corridor, as if she'd also become a ghost.

There were another three rooms besides those she knew about at her end of the corridor: two with bare mattresses, and one with sheets where they should be, tucked into the bed, with a coverlet on top. Wardrobes and chests of drawers were seemingly empty. Isla didn't even bother looking in them after the first room.

As she doubled back past Jessica's room, on her way to the other side of the house, she checked on her again. It was so still in her room, the only sound that of Jessica's breathing and the rain against the windows. Never had Isla known rain like this. It was relentless. Biblical, on occasion. If only it would turn to snow, it would lend some prettiness to surroundings that were otherwise so bleak.

Still in Jessica's room, she noticed the shadows that pooled in the corners. They'd multiplied, she was sure of it, recalling how the old woman had stared at them, clutching at her nightdress as she did, her eyes widening. But they were static shadows; nothing in them that moved forwards, even though she continued to gawp, half-expecting to see a figure of some sort, arms reaching further into the room, like children, wanting attention, demanding it. *Dead children.*

*Isla!*

What was she now? A horror writer instead of a carer?

*Just…get on with something more meaningful.*

What she was doing – exploring – could it be described as meaningful? Nosey, perhaps, but nothing more than that. *You're trying to gain an insight into your client.* Find some personality somewhere, rather than a stranger who was also strange.

As she walked, she wondered. Did her own room have shadows similar to those in Jessica's room? She'd tried not to notice them, last night or this morning – previously so tired, and later groggy with the start of a cold. Maybe she should peer harder at them tonight, or…she'd just shut her eyes and drift. That would be the best option. She shouldn't encourage anything, certainly not fantasies.

More bedrooms, another bathroom. What an incredible house this used to be, with its library, and fireplaces, and chandeliers. What a wreck it had turned into.

Again, she searched through a chest of drawers, but only briefly, finding nothing, only more dust that rose into the air at her touch, irritating her throat further and bringing on another coughing fit causing her to double over and clutch at her sides.

She turned around and eyed the bed, metal-framed and heavy. Despite its bare mattress, she could climb onto it, right now, and sleep, her bones weighing her down. She felt like she'd aged dramatically. No lightness of being, it had all been sucked from her, by the house, its lone occupant, and the vampiric *loneliness.*

*Lightness of being?*

Who was she kidding? It wasn't the house that was responsible, but her family. They'd never understood her.

Not in recent years, anyway.

Approaching the door, she exited the room. There was only one other room left to explore, that at the far end of the corridor. After that…well, after that, she'd best wake up Jessica, try to coax her to eat something, to sip some water, to visit the bathroom too. If not, if Jessica refused on all counts, then perhaps she'd sit with her again, take her by the hand, do what a carer was supposed to do, and just…care. Another wry smile appeared on her lips. *Practice makes perfect!* That smile abruptly disappeared as another thought chased it down. *You? Perfect? As if!*

This part of the house felt different from the other side, the atmosphere congealed, like the gravy of the beef stew she'd had earlier. If there was unease in her stomach, butterflies still, it was getting worse – causing her, once she'd reached the corridor, to turn, wanting to flee back down the stairs, and out of the front door. *Like that other one. Because you're no good, that's why. No good at anything.*

No! She wouldn't do it. She couldn't leave Jessica before further help could be arranged. But what she could do was return to the kitchen, drink some water and just…calm down, act like the adult she was supposed to be. 'Grow up.' Those words had been said to her on many occasions. 'And take some responsibility for once.'

*I'm doing it now, aren't I?* Maybe that's what all this working as a carer business was about. Because she was *desperate* to prove her worth. And yet her family didn't know how hard she was trying. She'd left no forwarding address.

The door to the last room was in front of her. She stood before it, until what seemed like an age had passed. Any bravery she had felt was now evaporating.

Why did it take bravery, though, to open another door?

Before she took a step closer, she listened out. Would anything scamper behind her? Or an echo of laughter erupt?

It was just another room. Something she kept telling herself as she reached out. The final one. After that, there'd be no more mystery regarding what lay beyond anything. If she didn't do this and check, then an imagination that had already gone into overdrive could push itself up another gear. One more room. Nothing to worry about. *The house is empty besides us.*

And yet that echo of laughter she'd heard… That scamper…

Before she could stop herself, she grabbed the door handle and opened it, half-expecting it to resist but not quite knowing why it should. Unlike some of the doors to other rooms, it didn't. It flew open under such force, almost as if it had been waiting to do just that. What she saw caused her once again to gasp, this time in wonder.

Yes, it was dusty. Cobwebs still hung from the ceiling, but unlike the other rooms, there was so much…*life* in this one. A children's room, she quickly realised. Two single beds in there, pushed against opposite walls. A pink throw on one, blue on the other. *Amelia and Gabriel's beds.* They had to be. There were toys…everywhere. On a series of shelves, on a rug in the middle of the floor, and spilling over the sides of several wooden chests. *Their* toys, the children romanticised in the portraits? There were no photographs, no more portraits, the house remaining stubbornly secretive, giving only so much away. All she could do was presume. But whoever these children were, they'd been loved, it was clear to see. They'd been lavished upon.

As she entered the room, her laughter was the thing that echoed. There, in an alcove by the window, was a Christmas tree! Decorations hanging from each bough. An artificial tree, but as brittle as if it were a real one that had dried out.

She drew nearer, her eyes as wide as any child's. All the decorations appeared to be of the homemade variety. Glittery things – at one time in their history anyway. They would have been colourful, some more sophisticated than others, but all naïve. Pretty, though, beneath the dust that covered them. As frail as Jessica.

1960 was when the children had died. *If* they were the children that had once occupied this bedroom, those in the portrait. The orphans. Brought to Wildacre, to be loved and adored. Isla spun around, surveying the room a second time. They had *everything* they could have wanted! A veritable mansion to call a home, a room such as this, sizeable with its high ceiling, giving the impression of yet more space. They could have had separate rooms, she supposed, but kids loved to share when they were young. She'd done so with her siblings, snuck into their beds whenever they'd let her. Her older siblings, because she was the youngest by a good few years. A surprise baby. A gift, her mother had said. An accident.

Wandering over to the mantlepiece that presided over another empty grate, the marble pale instead of black, she picked up an ornament. A porcelain figurine – a maid of some sort, similar to that she'd seen in a film, *Toy Story*, the Little Bo Peep character. A key poked out from the back of her. A music box?

Isla turned the key, exhibiting more childish delight. She could just imagine Amelia or Gabriel doing this, turning the key, keen to listen to a sweet lullaby. She'd had a music box when she'd been younger. She would lift the lid and there within it was a tiny ballerina set against a mirrored inlay, on

58

tiptoes, her hands gracefully arched. As the music played –
*Swan Lake* – the ballerina would twirl round and around. In
the box itself, she kept jewellery. Not anything expensive –
her family had no money for that – just plastic pieces, but
how she'd loved them. Anything bright, anything shiny.
Garish, her father would say, but back then she hadn't
known the meaning of the word. She'd adorn her neck and
hands in the jewellery, grab a pink feather boa she had too,
just a cheap dress-up piece, slip on a pair of her mother's
heels, and she'd dance and dance to the music, humming it
in her head long after the tune had finished. Everyone would
laugh as she gave such performances. 'That's her,' they'd say.
'Our Isla. Such an entertainer.' And she'd *love* the attention,
making people laugh, seeing how they'd wrinkle their noses,
shake their heads, and smile.

Happy times. The best. A childhood full of love. *That's
our Isla. That's our Isla. That's our Isla.* Everybody loves a
child. Everybody makes *allowances* for a child. But if such
gregarious behaviour follows you into later years, then
suddenly attitudes change – *bewilderingly* fast. Disdain
instead of delight. Disapproval.

The music the figurine was playing – not a tune she
recognised – ended, the sound of the battering rain
returned.

Tears filled her eyes as she continued to stand there,
clutching it, but she blinked them back. It was lovely to find
a room like this at Wildacre! A hint of its background. But
also sad, because that background was lost, and in the wake
of happiness, despair.

Not just a room, *a shrine.*

Everything kept the way it was when… She hesitated.
When what? Had it been an illness or an accident?

"What the fu—"

Music from the figurine burst into life again, although she hadn't turned the key. *Loud* music, not the gentle tinkling of before.

It wasn't that, however, that caused her to drop it, the porcelain as delicate as the decorations on the tree, and shattering instantly when it met the floor.

It wasn't the echoing laughter that she'd heard either, the same sound as before, that two children might make when engaged in a game together.

It was the roar that accompanied both sounds. Deep, guttural, and filled with fury, originating from further down the hallway, but hurtling its way towards her.

# Chapter Seven

## 22<sup>nd</sup> December

"It's Christmas, isn't it? It's that time of year…again?"

After what she'd experienced, Isla had no idea how she was carrying on. Was it something similar – that disembodied howl of rage – that the previous carer had heard, that strange echoing laughter too, causing them to flee? If so, then they *definitely* couldn't be blamed. And yet she, Isla Barrow, had heard it too and was still there. Looking after Jessica Lockhart. In a house that was…haunted?

All that had happened had been over in seconds. The music from the figurine silenced as soon as it had smashed. The collision had also silenced the laughter and the howl, the beating of her galloping heart taking over.

She'd clung to the mantlepiece, just so worried her legs would give way. There was no mirror hanging over the top of it as was so often the case, and she was grateful for that. She neither wanted to see her own horrified expression, nor what could be in the doorway behind her. Amelia and Gabriel? But that other voice, the more guttural one – that belonged to a monster, not a child. Who, though, she wondered, remembering that unmarked mound beside the children's graves.

Regarding the figurine, could it be some kind of technical fault? And that other stuff – the laughter, and the howl – was that just the wind finding its way in through various nooks and crannies, soughing through the eaves? There *had* to be logical explanations for it all. Isla simply didn't believe in ghosts. Who did? No one she knew. That kind of thing wasn't on her radar. And why would it be? She'd grown up in an ordinary house, that was lively, and far more modern in comparison to this one. Ghosts were the stuff of horror movies, of fiction; a bit of fun, something to give you a thrill and set your pulse racing. At Wildacre, though, so large and so empty, filled with white sheets and dust – with a shrine! – it was all too easy to believe in something *other* than what you could see. To get carried away with it all.

When she'd finally faced the doorway, the space was still empty. No crazy ghost glared at her. And she had a client to tend to. *And no flipping phone to call for help.* Had she really expected to find one? More and more she realised this was a house that had purposely cut itself off from civilisation, a house that wanted nothing to do with what lay outside it. No way Jessica Lockhart had a mobile phone secreted either, so who arranged her care? A friend or relative, it had to be. But from afar.

And now here she was – Jessica – asking whether it was that time of year again, Christmas.

Although Isla didn't know too much about dementia patients, she realised they had periods of lucidity. Having walked into Jessica's room, with oxtail soup, more tea and more water, she was stunned to find her sitting up, not glazed but expectant.

"You're…feeling better?" she'd said.

Jessica had nodded. "I'm fine. Who are you?"

"I've told you, I'm the carer, sent from the agency to look after you."

As Jessica placed the tray on the space she'd cleared previously on the dressing table, Jessica frowned, causing myriad more wrinkles. "The agency?"

"Marlin's Agency," Isla further explained, before seizing her chance, "Can I just check again? Is there a working landline here? I can't find one, but… Or a mobile?"

"A mobile?"

"Yes." Reaching into her rear pocket, Isla withdrew her own useless phone, kept with her for reasons of comfort, she supposed, the vain hope that it would burst back into life again, and waved it in the air for Jessica to see. "One of these."

Jessica shook her head. "Oh no. No."

"Then who organises your care? Would you be able to tell me their name?"

"I don't know who."

Damn it. She wasn't so lucid after all.

With the bowl of soup in hand, Isla brought it over to Jessica. "Look, you really must eat," she said. "I've also got some more tea for you."

Still, the woman refused, shaking her head almost violently.

Isla was at a loss what to do, how to handle this increasingly-changing situation.

*Just talk to her. Sit by her bed and talk.* To hell with whether she was lucid or not.

Placing the soup on the bedside table, hoping to entice her with it a bit later, she sat down, racking a mind that had annoyingly gone blank for something to say. That was when

63

Jessica had asked about Christmas, saving her the trouble.

"Yes, yes, it is," Isla replied. "It's December 22nd. Christmas is in three days."

"Three days?" Jessica clutched at her nightdress again. "So close."

"Jessica—"

"I used to love Christmas. Do you? Love it, I mean."

"I… Well…"

"It's a simple enough question. Do you?"

Isla was taken aback by the sudden demanding note in Jessica's voice.

"I don't really think about Christmas," she admitted. "Not nowadays."

"You don't *think* about it?"

"Because… Because…" God, she wished she could get the words out! *Because it used to be a happy time, but not anymore. It's lonely, as lonely as it seems to be here, at Wildacre. Not just another day, as some people insist, it's a day that makes you feel even worse than you did before, even…guiltier. It's a shitty day for me now, so no, I don't think about it. I do everything I can not to.* All this was on the tip of her tongue, but, of course, she wouldn't give voice to it. Jessica was her client but also a stranger, not someone to confide in just because she asked a pertinent question.

"I do like Christmas," she said instead. "I should imagine Christmas at Wildacre was very special."

Jessica smiled, and it was like a ray of sunlight, giving life to eyes that had previously been empty or confused. The blue of them was almost silvery. A pretty woman, Isla realised, in her younger days before time and perhaps tragedy had taken its toll. It was still there when she smiled, the merest hint, hiding behind skin that had become like parchment. A woman with children, *a history*. And a husband, there must have been. They would *all* have enjoyed Christmas here. Wouldn't they? *Let me into your world, Jessica, this world that I've stumbled on.*

Her wish was answered. Jessica began talking…*really talking*. Isla sat back in her chair to listen, to soak it all up. Everything she had to say.

"The house used to ring with laughter at Christmas! They loved it, you know, the children. We all did. Ah, such fun times…perfect! We would lavish them with gifts. But, tell me, who doesn't want to spoil their children? That's what you have them for, isn't it? Don't you agree? And Christmas… It isn't a time for sensibility, to hold back."

"The children—" Isla began, wanting to mention them by name, but Jessica was caught in the moment, reliving what was past.

"One Christmas morning, we woke, and it was snowing outside. Oh, I know that's not so unusual. We get so much snow in winter, into spring sometimes. In March and April too. But this time, on Christmas Eve, there'd been no hint of it. I'd gone to bed late, so late, and the night was black. And yet in the morning, there it was. Snow! The children loved it. They adored it. As soon as we'd all had breakfast, we donned coats, hats and gloves, went out to play in it. It was more exciting than receiving presents. We got so cold! But there was a roaring fire to return to, which we sat around afterwards, drinking mugs of cocoa. Perfect! Perfect! Perfect!"

The picture she'd painted was an ideal one, as romantic and as dreamy as the portraits downstairs. The late 50s was a long time ago, at least to Isla, but she found herself thinking Jessica was speaking about an age even further back than that — a time not characterised by any form of technology. *Ruined* by it. Although Isla was used to a switched-on world, Jessica, and Wildacre itself, were making it all too easy to picture something other. To prefer the simplicity of it, even.

"Presents weren't opened in the morning," Jessica continued. "Oh no, no, no. We did that early evening, the anticipation building and building as the day went on, making the most of it! What a lovely lunch we'd have! A roast dinner, roast potatoes, and vegetables. I'd cook it myself and to such applause! I can smell it now, roast lamb and roast beef, can you? The aroma that would fill the house, our stomachs growling with hunger. And then, once dinner was over, there'd be a plum pudding lit with brandy, the flames dancing! We'd retire to the living room, to the Christmas tree there, one so tall it touched the ceiling, gifts galore beneath it. And so the day would continue, the fun and the excitement, squeals from the children as they held a brand new doll, or a bright shiny car. Their eyes! Such delight in them."

"It all sounds...wonderful," Isla breathed when at last Jessica paused. "I can imagine it. The fun you said you had."

Jessica turned her head to her, and as before, the movement was viper-quick for a woman of her age and frailty. "Can you?" she said, and her tone, from being so vibrant, now had an edge to it. "Can you imagine it *all*? Every bit?"

"Jessica?" Isla responded, noting the woman's eyes were glazing. "I think you should lie back now. Get some rest—"

"A wonderful time," Jessica reiterated, but there was no conviction behind that statement now, *no belief*, it seemed.

"It was! It was!"

"Jessica," Isla said, rising to tend to her, "I don't doubt it. Why should I?"

"Do you like Christmas?"

From being so happy, her expression beatific, she was now agitated: the Jessica Lockhart that Isla knew and was growing used to. Before answering, Isla found herself swallowing hard. "I've told you, remember? I do like it." *Once upon a time it was as special as yours, in its own way.* "Now come on, rest up. Never mind the soup for now, have some water, that's it. Just a sip, Jessica. Here, let me help you."

Having grabbed the glass from the dressing table, she brought it back, and raised it determinedly to Jessica's lips. Before it touched her mouth, however, Jessica lifted her arm. Isla anticipated it this time and lifted her own arm higher, preventing Jessica from knocking the glass from her hands and soaking the bedclothes again.

"Jessica, you need to stop that—"

"You can imagine it all," Jessica repeated, her arms coming around herself now to hug her thin frame, her body rocking slightly. "Well, you can't! You could never imagine what it was like here. How different it was. Who even are you? A chit of a girl. What are you doing here? I don't understand. This is my house. Mine!"

"Jessica, I know that," Isla said, continuing to calm her. "Please lie back."

Jessica still refused. "What's left in this house is mine."

"Yes, I hear you. And it's true. Of course it's true."

"You can't just come in here," Jessica said, rocking more violently.

"I'm your carer," Isla reiterated.

"You can't just…*lay claim*."

"I'm not trying to. I would never—"

"I won't let you take them from me."

"Take who, Jessica? I don't understand—"

"Why do you keep calling me that?"

"Calling you what?"

"Jessica."

Isla had to stifle a sigh of exasperation. This was going from bad to worse. "Because that's your name. You're Jessica Lockhart, and this house is Wildacre."

"This house is *mine*," she said again, such seething in her voice, a wildness too. "You won't take it from me. Never. You won't take *them*."

# Chapter Eight

## 22<sup>nd</sup> December

What light there'd been that day had long since waned. The night was back in its entirety, and there was no let-up with the rain. Thank God *she'd* let up, though, Jessica. She'd had a period of remarkable lucidity, then an outburst, vehemently accusing Isla of wanting to steal from her, this house of all things, not growing used to Isla as her carer at all. Oh, how terrifying life must be, living with such confusion. Dementia was an awful disease that could strike anyone, maybe even lying in wait for Isla too one day – cutting her off from life even more than she was now.

Once Jessica had calmed, and was sleeping, Isla returned to her self-imposed cleaning duties. As well as the kitchen, she'd also washed surfaces in the main living room, wishing there was a TV or a radio in there, anything to give relief from the drumming of the rain against the windows, but no, there was nothing of the sort. When Jessica had said it was different at Wildacre, she wasn't joking.

Mostly she was just smearing dust from place to place, there simply being too much of it. It remained dull, nothing to hint at what Jessica had described, the cosiness of it, the towering Christmas tree, a warm fire. A losing battle.

And yet what else could she do but continue to fight it?

The next day, she *had* to go out again: head in the opposite direction and find someone with a link to the outside world. Jessica needed professional help, maybe even a hospital bed. Curiously, despite the dismay Isla felt at her efforts, she found she didn't *want* to go out; she was far from relishing the prospect. Her coughing had thankfully eased this afternoon, but her chest, throat and back were still achingly sore, her head pounded, and her forehead and cheeks were no longer cool but flushed with heat. Maybe she had indeed developed a fever.

Her eyes lingered on the grate. Oh, for it to be blazing right now! Gathering logs would be another job for the following day. There had to be matches somewhere in this house. She'd open every damned drawer in existence until she found them.

"Christ, what a mess we're in," she muttered under her breath, she and Jessica. Two strangers whose lives had become entwined. How to untangle themselves from each other, and remove the burden that had become Isla's, was still unclear.

Again, she thought of what Jessica had told her, and the things she'd described. There'd been such laughter in this room, such delight. Experienced everywhere in the house, Isla would bet, all the joy that a young family could bring. Hard to imagine it, though. It had left no impression on the atmosphere. What had come after it – although Isla could only suppose this – but the grief of loss, the thing to dominate.

*And anger too, Isla. Remember that roar? There's anger here.*

She was right. There *was* anger here, like the dust, blanketing everything. Jessica's anger? At whom, though?

Or was the anger attributable to someone else? Jessica must have had a husband. In Isla's day and age, being a single mother wasn't out of the ordinary, but back then it was nothing less than a crime. And the scene she'd described, it had seemed so family-orientated, although she hadn't mentioned a husband, or indeed the children's names. Had she adopted them? Were they the orphans she'd mentioned? So many questions, so much…mystery.

Mystery that was making her head pound even more. She'd done what she could for today, feeling so weary again. One thing she wasn't was hungry, a blessing in disguise being as there was nothing appetising in the kitchen. She'd take a hot drink to bed, though, check in on Jessica again, then hopefully get some sleep herself.

Jessica was awake when she entered her room, albeit barely, refusing to move when Isla suggested she help her to the bathroom. Defeated, she grabbed the remaining towels from there instead, and placed them under Jessica, hoping that if she had an accident, they'd soak up the worst of the mess. She then left her, wondering why she was worrying so much. The mattress was already soiled. She could *smell* the accidents it had borne, so it wasn't as if one more would make a difference. *Everything's ruined in this house,* she thought, making her way to her own bedroom. The hot drink she'd put there earlier would likely be tepid by now, but she had no desire to go back downstairs and turn on all the lights again, their pale shine barely penetrating the intensity of the darkness.

Intense… That certainly described this experience. Jessica's world had become Isla's. Everything other than what existed at Wildacre was now fading, a surprisingly easy groove to fall into. A groove that wouldn't last long, though.

71

It couldn't, not if Jessica was refusing to even drink anything. Soon she'd fade too, entirely.

Although wanting nothing more than to collapse on her bed, as dusty, as uninviting and as damp as it was, Isla headed to the bathroom to brush her teeth, seeing to the little things. These, too, were easy to forget at Wildacre, as if the rules of the outside world didn't apply. Here you just...made it all up as you went along.

Such a stark room. No colour in the bathroom to relieve the whiteness of the walls, the white tiles, the white sink, the white bath and the white window frames. A *grubby* white. *She* was the only thing to inject colour of any description, standing there in a faded pink tee-shirt and shorts. Staring into the mirror, as she'd done on the first night, she noted her cheeks were pink too, when usually she was winter-pale. She sighed. So she *was* feverish then, chills now and then making her shiver. In the end, brushing her teeth was a half-hearted attempt, due to exhaustion. A good night's sleep was definitely needed, Jessica hopefully remaining silent, as silent as the house, as silent as that hymn she used to sing at Christmas, *Silent Night*. She'd always loved those kinds of festive tunes, how they captured the melancholia of the season as well as the joy. Wildacre captured the melancholia, that was for sure, but there *had* been joy, and wonder, and excitement. And for a moment, in the children's room, and downstairs in the hallway when she'd first stared at their portraits, she'd heard the echoes of the laughter that used to exist.

*You heard no such thing!*

And even if she had, now was not the time to think of it, at night, in this house, when she and Jessica were alone.

She rinsed her mouth, then gave one final glance at her

reflection, noting the hollowness of her eyes, and the darkness of the circles that sat beneath them. *You look haunted.* And again she chided herself for such thoughts. There were no ghosts here, no dead children laughing, no roar of anger from another. *But the figurine, the music that had played…* Was a technical fault, and therefore logical, perfectly logical.

In the corridor, she looked first one way, towards the children's room, and then, more tentatively, in the opposite direction. That was where she'd imagined the roar to have come from earlier, the room at the far end of the same corridor she and Jessica occupied. A room she'd stood on the threshold of, but nothing more. It was just like all the others: big and empty.

Perhaps some possessions remained, concealed. No way she'd check now, though, at this hour. Curious she may be, but she was not stupid.

Maybe the next day. Maybe not.

More coughing stole more energy. She needed sleep. Hopefully she'd feel better in the morning, because right now, it was like she also had one foot in the grave.

Entering her room, the lamp she'd previously turned on cast a glow that was more hostile than cosy. Were there shadows in the corners, as there were in Jessica's room? *Don't look,* she told herself. *Just go to bed and shut your eyes.*

She climbed between the sheets, immediately coughing as dust and the stench of mould assailed her. When she quieted, she found she was still breathing hard, her throat catching, refusing to settle. As much as she craved sleep, as exhausted as she was, would she be able to? Or would she lie awake all night, listening out for noises, to every creak and groan an old house made, imagining all the while…?

In the end, she succumbed easily to sleep, but it was feverish. She was dreaming, and part of her brain was perfectly aware of that. Another jumble of dreams, though. The shadows in the corners – were they there? Reaching out for her? And was she really sitting up in bed and reaching back? Who were they?

"Amelia? Gabriel?"

Was she calling out their names too?

When she next surfaced, she was lying in the foetal position, not sitting up at all. There was that scampering sound. Footsteps passing by her door, light and quick, *running* down the hallway. In which direction? She listened harder, but it was as if she was being pushed back into dreams, them not willing to let her go yet.

There were murmurs too, a deeper voice than Jessica's, the sound of a man talking. Then there'd be laughter, from both a male and female, short bursts of it. Not a nightmare at all! It was pleasant to listen to. Initially. But then the laughter took on a different quality, with a more manic edge to it. No more conversation. There was shouting, and suddenly, with absolute certainty, Isla knew she'd hear it: that roar, fuelled by rage. In her dream-like state, she'd braced herself for it.

Such laughter at Wildacre. Such fury. How had it swung from one to the other?

Whimpering. Was that a child crying? Two children? A vision of them entered her head, wispy, just as the portraits of them were wispy. The pair of them were huddled together. Not in their bedroom. They were at the top of the stairs, listening to what was happening around them. The argument. The fight. The threats.

*The deterioration.*

74

Her heart was racing; she noticed that too. Because this world she'd entered, one that existed deep within another, *was* threatening. The air was heavy with it. Was she in danger, though? This was only a dream, and therefore danger should disappear as soon as you woke. Despite telling herself this, dread only increased.

*Wake up, Isla! Wake up!*

She was doing her utmost, trying to swap the subconscious for the conscious. Force the issue, like she'd done so many times before when dreams had taken a sinister turn. Sinister? Yes, that described exactly what was happening here, further prompting her to try and claw her way out of it, like a swimmer deep in the ocean, propelling herself ever upwards towards a spot of light that glimmered above her.

Footsteps again. That heavier tread. These ones were not outside her door, but distant, although drawing nearer. Perhaps whoever was responsible for them was climbing the staircase? Once they'd reached the top, which way would they turn? Towards the children's bedroom – the shrine? Or head towards her and Jessica?

The footsteps stopped. So they'd reached the top, and were possibly deciding which way to go. What if it was a real-life intruder, and here she was, stuck in dreams, unable to protect Jessica, or herself?

When she'd first arrived at Wildacre, the door was unlocked. Which was just as well, because she could find no key safe. But that's what people in the countryside did – they left their doors unlocked. She knew that; she'd been told that. They did so because out here nobody intruded. The countryside, especially one as barren as this, was supposed to be safe. But what if it wasn't? This was a large house.

Someone other than Jessica could have been here all along – maybe that's what had scared the other carer. But if so, surely they would have mentioned that to their manager, or called the police?

Oh, who was it out there? Which way would they turn? Why couldn't she wake up? How come it didn't seem like she was dreaming, but real?

The footsteps restarted. Whoever it was – an intruder, a ghost or a dream-conjured figure – was coming towards her.

She couldn't breathe, felt more feverish. There was no healing in sleep; rather, it had plunged her further into delirium. There was no one else in the house, this was just a dream, but whoever was responsible, their *determination*, was unmistakable.

A falter again, between her door and Jessica's. Her throat tickled. She was going to cough, but she mustn't. She had to keep quiet – or whoever it was, and no matter if it was just a dream figure, would burst right in there, their eyes bulging and their mouth cavern-like as they roared. They'd come for her. To *destroy* her.

*Don't cough! Don't cough! Don't!*

She heard herself splutter instead as she forced the cough back. She then turned her head, as some movement in the room caught her dream sight.

As she'd thought earlier, someone was reaching out from the shadows. One set of arms. Two sets. Something so pitiful about the movement.

*I can't help you. Not now.*

But still they begged her, whoever *they* were.

*Stay where you are, in the shadows. Someone's out there. Someone's…listening.*

Another footstep, just the one, towards her door.

*Go away! Go away! Go away!*

That was the mantra now in Isla's head. The prayer of the desperate.

*Please go away.*

Breath escaped her as the footsteps continued down the corridor, *all* the way down it seemed, growing fainter.

Another moment of silence. The dream was over, surely? She looked towards the corner, but saw no arms protruding. They too had gone. She could surface now, safely. And once she'd surfaced, laugh at herself, at how scared she'd become, her heart rate no doubt taking its own sweet time to slow.

The next minute, her heart almost burst from her chest.

There *was* someone. They were banging on the door down there! The sound reverberated through the house. Then the roar she dreaded, and screaming too.

Adrenalin flooding her, she jumped from the bed, definitely awake now, and moved towards the door, almost slipping in her haste, and crashing to the floor. She had to see what was going on, because not knowing was worse. Confront whomever it was. Demand that they leave here, or what? She'd call the police? If only.

Just before yanking at the door, her gaze returned to the corner. Something of the dream lingered. For although they weren't reaching out, she saw two children, as before. Amelia and Gabriel were there still, huddled together, and shaking.

# Chapter Nine

## 23<sup>rd</sup> December

"That's it, place this blanket over your knees. That will also help to keep you warm."

Isla had managed it. She'd got Jessica downstairs. The woman was lucid this morning; compliant, but quiet. She'd *wanted* to come downstairs. Had asked to.

'It's time,' she'd said, 'almost time.'

If she was surprised to enter the room and find furniture on show rather than being covered, Jessica gave no hint. She simply sat on the sofa in front of a fire that Isla had earlier prepared, having indeed found logs in an outhouse in the grounds – a whole heap of them, and some dry despite the leaking roof. She'd carried them back to the house and positioned them in the grate, resolving to fetch more later, and now flames were beginning to hiss. Isla was hoping they'd soon catch, become more robust, take the edge of this cold that wouldn't subside, and do the job the ancient radiators couldn't. She'd also brought more water and soup in from the kitchen. To her relief, Jessica had taken a few sips of water and a mouthful of soup, but then refused any more. *Not enough to keep body and soul together.* The woman was dying, and there didn't seem to be a thing she could do to stop it.

As she sat too, in an armchair next to the sofa, she, like Jessica, gazed at the fire. Not long past 11am, yet it felt so much later. She was tired, surreptitiously rubbing at her eyes. Some coffee she'd drunk earlier, *stale* coffee, had failed to give her the energy boost she needed. After being awake most of the night, then finding those logs and hauling them in, and seeing to Jessica, she felt more feverish than ever. She wanted to sleep, to close her eyes, right there on the armchair, and drift off, but dreams were proving a double-edged sword at Wildacre.

Dreams… Those footsteps she'd heard, so determined, the children she'd seen in the corner, huddling, frightened, and then…the banging on the bedroom door at the end of the hallway, the roaring and the screaming. It had all succeeded in dragging her out of bed at last, awake, definitely awake, when previously she'd only thought she was. She'd gone rushing into the corridor outside, not knowing what she'd encounter – possibly an intruder, one she'd be at the mercy of, as she had no weapon to fend them off. Maybe even two of them; a man and a woman it had sounded like. All she knew was she had to do something. She couldn't just lie there, listening to such catastrophe. She also had Jessica, a vulnerable woman, to think of.

The screams had torn at the atmosphere. And yet as soon as her bare feet had touched that threadbare runner outside her room, there was nothing. Only silence, and a gloom that was thicker than ever.

Her chest heaving, coughing again, she'd stood there, bewildered. A dream, after all, she'd concluded. The fever she was suffering, that had come on so suddenly, was responsible for blurring the lines between reality and illusion.

Still she'd continued to stand there, shivering. She'd always wondered what it might be like to live in a house as grand as this. Who hadn't? But it was *not* a grand house, not any more. It was full of dust and grime and cobwebs, of past lives suppressed, trying to break free. The sooner she left, the better. Despite how ill she felt, and how ill Jessica was, she'd go in the morning, walk in the other direction as planned, and find someone to help. No matter if it was raining still; even if thunder and lightning returned, she'd do it. When she thought about it, the weather was like an expression of the torment occurring inside the house, inside both its occupants too.

It was the sound of movement which again galvanised her. Not coming from further down the corridor – the room at the end that the heavier footsteps had hurried to – but from Jessica's room. She was awake, in the dead of night, just as Isla was. She must go in there, tend to her, take her to the bathroom, try to get her to sip some water. *The same old routine,* she thought wryly, already too used to the futility of it. As she forced life back into her limbs to head there, fear gripped her again – another aspect of the daily routine. What if the movement inside that room wasn't caused by Jessica? What if the shadows were responsible? Moving out of the umbra and towards her, growing bolder? This time of year…it was the darkest time of year, blue skies something of a memory too, those long days of summer that you thought might last forever. *That's why there's Christmas, why we light up the season.* She'd often thought about that. To celebrate the birth of Jesus was the Christian reasoning, but before that, in older times, had there been another? You lit up the season because you had to. It was only light that kept the shadows at bay. *Repelled them.* But there was so very little light at Wildacre. Hardly any life, and no hope it seemed. And *that* was why the shadows were able to break free, because nothing held them back.

All she'd wanted was to return to her own room, dive under the sheets and blankets, pull them up over her head and stay there till morning, come what may. But she pushed open the door Jessica's room, albeit with such trepidation.

When at last she could see inside, she sighed with relief. There were no shadows congregating around Jessica's bed. She felt stupid for even thinking it. But Jessica was sitting up, facing her. Her expression, in the glow of the lamp that Isla had left on, was ravaged.

Before Isla could rush to her and ask what the matter was, Jessica had spoken.

"I know."

Two words. Simple words, ordinary, but they'd made Isla shiver further.

"You know?" she'd said, as she made her way over. "You…heard?"

Jessica hadn't said anything more – neither confirmed nor denied it. Like a wraith from the grave, she had risen from the bed, approaching Isla on perfectly steady feet. She'd glided past her and into the corridor, and stood in the very spot Isla had occupied, gazing in the direction of the room at the end, where the screams had finally erupted. Isla stared after her, bewildered once again. And then…she'd crumpled. Isla darted forwards, catching her before she could hit the floor. A wraith she'd likened her to, and she'd been right; she was a woman of very little physical substance. But mentally, Isla suspected, she carried an enormous load.

She'd helped her to the bathroom, got her into bed, and then finally returned to her own room, there to lie awake for the rest of the night, sometimes quietly, sometimes coughing, the dawn taking forever to arrive. But during that time, she enhanced her plan further. She wouldn't only check for a house in the opposite direction, she'd also inject some life back into this house, just at the point that life was becoming extinct. Jessica had walked perfectly well earlier, showing she'd once been a self-sufficient woman. But if she didn't eat… If she didn't drink…

*The end is coming.* Isla returned to the present, to the living room they were both in. Jessica had closed her eyes, to doze in front of a fire that had indeed burst into life. The room was feeling cosy at last, *almost* cosy, when it had been so drab – extraordinary how a fire could make such a difference. Even so, Isla knew – with something like extreme certainty – that she was right in thinking what she had.

The end was coming for Jessica Lockhart, lone resident of Wildacre. And Isla was damned if she wouldn't make that end as comfortable as possible.

Atonement. There it was, handed to her, the possibility of it.

And, considering the time of year, a gift.

* * *

Wanting to doze, like Jessica, but fighting against it, Isla listened out instead for the sound of scampering feet, echoes of laughter, or a shrill scream. There was nothing, of course, just the crackling of the fire, the rhythm as soporific as the heat. Again, she wondered what would become of this house after its last occupant was no longer here. Or maybe she was being too maudlin. The house, the situation she was in, and her illness, were all bringing her down way too much. And

Jessica wouldn't die – not if Isla could find help for her, *proper* help. She'd recover from her present state.

She did doze eventually, something she only realised when she woke, startled by something. What it was, though, she had no idea. Footsteps, after all?

"Jessica? Jessica, are you okay?"

Her sudden fright that it was Jessica was quickly calmed. She was right there, in front of her, on the sofa, still asleep. The fire, though, had died down.

*Shit, what time is it?*

She checked her watch. Nearly 2 pm. Quickly, she worked it out. She'd slept for two hours! How? *Because you're exhausted, Isla! You're ill. That's how.* She needed to head on up the road whilst there was still some daylight left.

It seemed to have made no difference that she'd slept. She was as tired as ever, unsure again if her legs would support her as she rose.

Despite her misgivings, she made her way over to Jessica steadily enough, and gently roused her. The woman stirred, opened her rheumy eyes. There was no silver in them at all now. Isla tried to tempt her to drink some more water, but was rebuffed.

"No," she was murmuring, "sleep. Just sleep."

As she'd helped her downstairs, she helped her back upstairs, wondering if she'd linger at the portraits of the children. But, as she'd done on the way to the living room, Jessica kept her gaze averted, although Isla was sure that something in her stiffened, causing the woman to lean more heavily on her.

Back in her bedroom, Jessica settled easily, her breathing becoming deeper and more even.

Isla sat with Jessica, just for a short while, tried to breathe evenly too, although not deeply as that would set off the coughing. Could she do this? Leave the house? Go in search of someone? She was indeed becoming housebound, if only by proxy. A thought that didn't sit comfortably, that feeling that once you'd entered this house, it ensnared you, the wind and rain peculiar only to the land that Wildacre was on. Elsewhere, it might already have turned to snow, transforming itself from something treacherous into something magical that brought so much joy. It *had* brought joy here, when the children were alive. But all joy was gone.

As much as she wanted to lie down beside Jessica on a bed that was soiled, whose smell she'd got used to, just as she was getting used to everything else around here, the strangeness of it, she pushed herself to her feet instead, rubbing at her eyes, knowing how red-rimmed they were. Mindful of the fading light, she hurried as fast as she could, out of the room and downstairs, past the portraits, across the hallway, and into the porch where her coat and boots were. Suitably dressed, she ventured back into the rain, yelping at the coldness of it against her cheeks.

Tears on her face mingled with the rain, and she coughed and sniffed, coughed and sniffed, trudging past the stone urns, forcing herself down that gravel driveway.

On the road, she veered right instead of left. The tears were still coming, refusing to stop, and, after only a few paces, overwhelming her. She stopped, bent over, and held onto her stomach as if somehow the emotions she was experiencing were volcanic. *Hopeless.* There was that word again, tormenting her. *All this is hopeless. And it's no more than you deserve. Perhaps Jessica too.*

For how had it got that way, that a woman should die alone, dependent on paid care, with no one to help her other than the agency?

Was that to be her own fate, in the dim and distant future? She would die. Not today, nothing like that, but on another day to come, and just as lonely. In a tiny flat, rather than somewhere as fancy as Wildacre, a stranger in yet another town she didn't belong to. A loneliness that was self-inflicted, she reminded herself. That she'd brought on herself. *Because you had to. Because…you're a coward.*

"Walk, Isla! Walk! Walk! Walk!"

Still coughing, still crying, she straightened. If there was a house up there, some form of help, she could save one of them at least. Although all she could see ahead was lane and more lane, tall hedges obscuring everything either side of it.

"FUCK!" she screamed, frustration mounting. "Just fucking walk."

Other than her, there was no sound of life, just…plenty of nothing.

She should turn back. The light was already failing, and if Jessica should wake…

She *did* turn back, not once, but twice, each time persuading herself to turn back around and press on, not go home just yet. *Home.* Why on earth was she calling Wildacre that? Whatever it had been, it now only supported the most basic survival.

Rounding a corner, she could have punched the air in triumph. There was a house! At last. Far more modest than Wildacre, which was also a relief. At least she didn't have another big mansion to deal with, and owners perhaps equally as odd.

She checked her watch and tried to work out how much time had passed until she'd reached it. Fifteen minutes, twenty? So quickly time passed out here, and yet at other times, such as when she'd lain in bed during the early hours of this morning, waiting for the light of day, it dragged its heels.

Gloom surrounded the house in front of her. Although set in large grounds, it was much plainer than Wildacre, a far more recent build. That same gloom around it seemed to have penetrated the walls, as no lights shone from upstairs or downstairs. No matter; she'd draw closer and bang on the door. It could be she'd spot another house in the distance whilst doing so, the lane perhaps opening up.

There weren't any other houses, just this one, as far as she could see beyond the trees, anyway. There was no car in the driveway, which also rang alarm bells.

It was Christmas. People either stayed home for the season, or travelled to be with friends and family. Is that what had happened here? Or was whoever lived here simply at work, or shopping, and would return later? If so, how much later? Isla couldn't be gone from Jessica too long.

Maybe, just maybe, there *was* someone home. Could there be a light on at the rear of the property, that she couldn't see from where she was standing?

A plaque mounted to the wall beside the door identified the house as *Acre Lodge* in solid black writing. Isla took a deep, somewhat jagged breath and rang the bell, listening to the tone of it, which was far more robust than the bell at Wildacre. Despite this, no one came to the door. Next, Isla made a fist with her hand and knocked at the door, willing it to open, for a man or a woman to stand before her, a surprised but friendly enough smile on their face. Again, nothing.

Her feet stamped at the ground as she fought the cold and more despair. She wished she'd thought to bring a pen and a scrap of paper. If she had, she could have written a note, posted it through the letter box and begged for help that way. *Urgent. We're at Wildacre. Owner ill. Please send an ambulance.*

She moved towards a window, seeing the curtains left half-open, and peered in. What she saw caused her heart to plummet further and her mouth to open wide, to scream with the frustration of it all. "Shit! Shit! Shit!" More tears filled her eyes.

No use banging on the door, or attempt to make a return visit and leave a note. The house was a shell. Empty. Either up for sale (although no board showed that) or about to be moved into. *New year, new start.* But New Year was too far away.

She fell against the sill, her forehead touching the window pane, only vaguely acknowledging the contrast of the cool glass against her burning face.

All the energy she'd mustered to come here deserted her. She was spent. Defeated. The only option was to curl up as tightly as she'd wanted to earlier, close her eyes and drift, just as Jessica was drifting. Like her, go somewhere – anywhere – other than the disaster that was here.

Her back against the wall, she slid down it until she was sitting on the ground. The concrete was damp and unforgiving. Her head resting against the wall, she closed her eyes, the rain battering her face still but she hardly felt it, becoming numb instead. *That's better. So much better.* Despair really was so easy to embrace.

If she died here after all, would her spirit linger? Would she haunt this place for ever more? The new owners would be full of excitement at moving in, and then full of trepidation as she did what ghosts do: tormenting them, feeding on their fear – just as whatever was at Wildacre was feeding on hers, growing stronger because of it.

Oh, what did it matter? Wildacre was long gone. She could forget about it, forget about everything, drift… It was so tempting. A delicious prospect.

*Christmas Eve tomorrow, in a few hours, and I'll have died alone. And so will you, Jessica Lockhart. I can't help that, like I couldn't help what happened before, either. I didn't mean it to happen! Although I bet they think I did, that I don't care. So many die alone. It's just the way of it. Life gone. Quickly. So quickly. In a flash. But it doesn't matter. It really doesn't. Sleep. Die. That's the only atonement you can make. Sorry, though, Jessica. I am sorry…*

A cough that was more like a bark fought its way out of her mouth – sudden, unexpected, and overwhelming. She'd been asleep, just asleep, although it may well have turned into something deeper, into what she wanted, an effortless exit. But her body had rebelled, the cough doubling her over as it had done several times before, making her fight for breath when seconds before she hadn't wanted to breathe at all.

Gasping, coughing, she scrabbled to push herself upwards. It wasn't just gloomy any more; darkness was gaining a stronghold. With rain continuing to pelt down on her, she at last stood, and staggered forwards. *Go back to Wildacre. You promised yourself you'd make Jessica's remaining time as comfortable as possible. Stick to your promises for once! At least try!*

She forced herself forwards, the shock of what she'd just attempted making her shiver all the more. She felt like she was dying with flu, and yet it was the flu that had saved her. More and more irony. If she'd hadn't had another coughing fit, would she have been successful in her attempt, with hypothermia setting in, and proving fatal?

So close to death, craving it – twice in the past few days – she was now repulsed by her actions. More disappointed in herself than ever.

*Enough, Isla, just…stop it! You're a coward, you really are! And so, so selfish. Look after Jessica, do what it takes. Don't leave her alone again, not until…until…*

There was the driveway to the house ahead, those ivy-covered pillars visible. *I'm coming, Jessica. I'm here for you.* Because someone had to be. Paid or unpaid. Frightened or not. Not just frightened, *terrified*, to go back there, but ploughing on.

Christmas Eve was coming – Jessica's last Christmas.

*Make it special.*

She swapped tarmac for gravel. The house would soon come into sight. If only she'd thought to leave a light on downstairs, and not have to encounter it in darkness again. The urns, like three ghostly figures, loomed ahead of her. Her eyes trained on them, she stopped. Three urns. *Just* three. She knew that. There was nothing and no more surrounding them. And yet…were there another two figures besides them? Not as tall, or as robust, but smaller, more delicate?

Nothing as solid as stone. Something far wispier.

Her breath caught in her throat as she peered harder.

Three shapes, not five. She must have been mistaken. Again.

She trudged on, this time with her head lowered.

# Chapter Ten

## 23<sup>rd</sup> December

Joy! She'd searched and searched and at last found what she was looking for – alcohol. She didn't care what type it was, only that it'd do the trick. A bottle of whisky, three-quarters full, right at the back of one of the kitchen cupboards, hidden by a sea of tins. The dust on the glass was predictably thick, but no matter, she'd wipe it off, and drink what she needed to in order to sleep tonight. *Dreamlessly* sleep.

She'd seen to Jessica first, of course. The woman in one of her compliant moods, allowing Isla to wash and toilet her, but refusing anything other than the standard few sips of water. Isla felt both despair and relief about that. *Not long now,* she kept saying, but only in her head. *Not long and this will all be over.*

Quiet as the grave. That's what the house was like tonight. Isla was back in the living room, but on her own this time, with Jessica in bed upstairs. She'd attempted to make another fire in the grate, but the flames were struggling this time, Isla able to glean no real warmth from them. Outside, the rain seemed to have stopped, but what good was that when it was nighttime, and therefore prohibitive? No way she'd go out there, not when darkness lay so undisturbed, when she was all alone.

The whisky was proving as much a comfort as she'd hoped. Isla took swigs of it as she looked around the room, wondering – as she'd done before – where all the personal items were, those that were usually collected over a lifetime, what Jessica had done with them. And yet…the children's room lay undisturbed. There was an attic at Wildacre, of course. She'd seen the hatch for it upstairs, but she wasn't going there either. If that's where all that kind of stuff was stashed, then it could stay there.

With the glass at her mouth, she took another drag of whisky and closed her eyes. She felt the warmth of that at least, lacing her throat. If she drank enough, it'd also make the tinned food at her disposal more palatable: more stew, or a soup. As much as she wanted to drink herself into oblivion, she mustn't. She just had to take the edge of things. Rising, she found within herself the courage to explore the downstairs again, in case she'd missed something of any importance, and she'd take the bottle with her. Others had lived in this house besides Jessica. Children had. There must be some allusion to them other than the shrine and the portraits.

She left the room at last, and made her ways on legs that now felt spongy, she had to admit, into the hallway rather than the rooms opposite. Coming to a halt in front of the two paintings, she studied them again: the glamour of them, the muted colours that spoke of another age, the wistfulness, the painter succeeding in capturing a precious moment in time, and making it eternal.

Truly beautiful paintings, and – only now did she note this – there was no dust on their frames. Even in the dim light of the chandelier (a fitting that should blaze, given the number of bulbs it contained), the frames were not only dustless; they shone.

Had the previous carer been charged with the task of cleaning them, or was it something Jessica herself saw to? A woman who could walk, who could talk when she wanted to, who wasn't always as frail as she was now?

Still in the hallway, she noticed something else that was new, that made her close the gap between herself and the wall where the paintings were hanging. There was a space between them where another painting might hang. *Had* hung, she corrected, because there it was: an impression, an outline – faint, but definitely there. Who had the missing portrait depicted? Jessica and someone else? Her husband and the father of Amelia and Gabriel? The one that lay in the unmarked mound beside them? Why unmarked? And where was that painting? Also stowed away somewhere?

The discovery gave her new impetus. She should search harder, curious to see what the young Jessica would have looked like, the pretty woman she suspected her to be, and the man she'd loved and had started a family with, biological or otherwise.

She headed to the far side of the house, to the room she thought of as a study. Darting inside, her presence caused dust motes to perform a frenzied dance in the air. Pre-empting a bout of coughing, she took another glug of whisky to ease her throat, before heading to the desk and placing the bottle down.

It was a beautiful desk. The wood was solid, and a patterned inlay decorated the edges. Where, once upon a time, someone had sat, taken phone calls and written letters. No telephone now, though, as she already knew, and no evidence of any letters. A purge had taken place, for reasons known only to Jessica.

There were drawers in the desk, three on either side. Isla had searched these particular ones before, but she did so again, running her hands right around the back of each, looking for something that might have survived the clearout, either by design or by accident. Nothing. If Jessica had carried out such a task, she'd been thorough about it. Deflated, Isla sat in the chair that fitted beneath the desk, still covered by a sheet that flailed either side of her. If she gathered it up and pulled it over her head, she'd look like a cartoon ghost. That thought, probably because of the whisky, made her laugh rather than quake, as it had before.

What strange things rooms were, she thought, reaching for the bottle. Either bursting with life, or harbouring nothing but echoes. Seriously, how long had Jessica lived like this? Basically closing off the house and occupying only what was necessary. *At least she had a shrine to pray at.* Another morbid thought that caused a burst of laughter, although this time it had a much hollower ring to it. It was as if…Jessica had died too, and likely at about the same time as her children, in 1960.

She brought the bottle to her mouth. *Just sip it. Don't glug like last time.* Despite that instruction, the liquid poured down her throat, hard and fast. *Fuck what I did last time.* Here, in this house, 'last times' didn't exist. They'd been erased.

But the portrait – the very thing she'd been inspired to look for – had that remained? Only one way to find out.

On her feet, stirring up more dust, infinite amounts, she tore back every one of the remaining sheets and left them lying in a pile on the floor. No portrait there. She ran into the dining room and looked around. No obvious hiding place in that room either, or in the snug. Again, she bundled what white sheets she'd previously left, that acted as spectres, and put them in piles in corners. More normal, that's how it appeared, or as normal as it got at Wildacre. No personal items, no missing portrait, only furniture.

More laughter as she darted about, the whisky bottle a faithful friend. Dressed in boots, jeans, a tee shirt and woollen jumper, she wished suddenly for more formal clothing – the kind you'd wear to a party or a ball. Surely, this house had hosted parties and balls in the past? A travesty if not; it was made for it! If she was wearing such a dress, she'd whirl and twirl like a princess, dancing from room to room instead of running, pirouetting now as she was in the hallway, coming to a jagged halt in front of the portraits, imagining herself to be the subject of the one that was missing. She and another: a man, tall and dark and imposing. The man of her dreams, someone who'd ridden in and rescued her from the loneliness of Wildacre.

Yes, she was coughing as she danced, and yes, she was still feeling feverish, but she was also giddy with excitement, lost in these imaginings. Rather than go any further, she remained in the hallway, performing a deep curtsey. Once again a princess greeting her prince. She could hear music – faint strains – when previously there'd been only silence. Glugging more whisky, she placed the bottle down on that long narrow empty table that lined the wall. Only part of her registered how little of the liquid remained. The other part…not caring, too busy relishing some happiness, when happiness had eluded her for so long.

"Let the music play on," she said, giggling and coughing some more, carried away on the tide of it. Not modern music, the type she usually listened to. There were violins, flutes and piano, all blending seamlessly, a *romantic* tune, and therefore fitting. For there had been romance here once. There'd been love.

Her arms wrapped around her body, she was hugging herself, imagining they belonged to another, that she was being pulled into him, impossibly close, to the point where it was hard to tell where she ended and he began.

"This is love," she breathed, enraptured by it.

She knew it was, and yet…she was only twenty-four, and had never been in love before. Oh, she'd had boyfriends, but this was different. So much richer. *Orphans of the storm.* Part of that phrase came to mind again. *That's what we are. You and me. We only have each other now.* As confused as she felt by these words, the way they'd entered her mind and wouldn't fade, she focused only on the music, on his arms, on the love she felt, that swelled to match his. Because it *did* match, perfectly.

"I love you." Again, she breathed the words, her eyes closed, her head tilted back. No need to find that portrait, for she could imagine the man he'd been, how handsome he was. The most handsome man she'd ever seen, his hair so dark it was almost black, and eyes that shone solely for her. Soon she'd feel the touch of his lips on hers, his tongue probing. This was life. And it had happened here, in this very spot: two bodies entwined. The world outside meant nothing; it was but a mere distraction. All that mattered was at Wildacre, a world no one could encroach on.

Parties. There had been. But only for two. Wildacre was a refuge, where love, growing more intense, could flourish, creating more love. Creating…them.

Her eyes snapped open. There was no music. It had been another imagining. But this wasn't. The chandelier and wall scones were flickering as they'd done when she'd first entered the house, but this time *wildly* flickering. The sound of footsteps and laughter had ceased abruptly, to be replaced by frantic whisperings.

"Hello," she shouted, a definite slur in her voice. "Who's there? What's happening?"

The light kept rhythm with the pounding in her head, making her feel suddenly dizzy and nauseous. Arms that had hugged herself were now flung out to keep steady. What was going on? Was it caused by some kind of electrical fault? But the footsteps, the laughter… what could explain them? Echoes, replaying? The past not erased, but very much a part of the present.

She'd head to the light panel, flick the switches there and try to rectify this anomaly. Switches which were close to the door, the exit. Again, she thought it, *I should run, like the carer did, all the way back to Alnwick. Get away from here.*

No matter how much she might want that, in this moment particularly, she steered to the switches, not the door. But if she expected results as her hand worked, she didn't get them. The lights continued to flicker. If anything they were worse than before, making her eyes hurt as well as her head. She had to escape it and return to the living room, just until she decided what to do. Find a refuge within a refuge.

Halfway there, she stopped. No use going to the living room. If there was a fuse box, it would be in the kitchen. She had to find it, and flick that switch instead, or shut down the whole damned system if she had to. Even darkness was better than this.

With that in mind, she turned, took a deep breath, then screamed.

There was something in the flickering lights. Just

beyond. Visible, then not visible. There for a fraction of a moment, then quickly disappearing.

Unable to move, Isla could only stare. Who was it? *What* was it?

A figure. As tall as the man she'd been dreaming about. Either dressed in black, or appeared that way because he was merely a silhouette, a shadow that had wrenched itself free, and gained substance. He was staring right back at her, she'd swear it, the eyes she'd imagined shining solely for her now depthless orbs in which she wouldn't drown in rivers of pleasure, but thrash about in, screaming instead.

A figure that was…moving. For real? Or were the flickering lights making it seem so? Alcohol and a feverish mind enhancing everything. She shook her head, even though it caused a fresh burst of pain. No, it wasn't the fever, nor the whisky, it was this house. Wildacre was the thing that was making her ill, draining her, leaving her exhausted and confused. For this was confusion, surely? Another trick of the mind.

There was no one in the flickering lights. She was the only one there, she *and* Jessica. The house was empty but for them, devoid of everything.

Despite trying to convince herself of this, she could only inch her way towards the stairs, at the top of which was only darkness, nothing flickering at all. No way she could make it to the kitchen now, not when the way was barred.

No more shouting out. Instinctively, she knew to keep quiet. This thing was not an intruder of the normal variety, a burglar, someone who'd happened this way and found a house as vulnerable as its owner. This was something she'd never encountered before, although still her mind refused to entertain the word 'ghost', the concept of it. They didn't exist! It was madness to think otherwise. This house, though, *bred* madness. She hadn't felt sane since she'd entered its grounds. As for Jessica, she'd lost her mind too, a long time ago. Years ago. *Decades*, even.

Having reached the foot of the staircase, some part of her amazed that he – whoever he was – had allowed her to get that far, she placed her foot on the bottom step, flailing for the bannister all the while. As her hand enclosed, it wasn't warm to the touch, as wood usually was – but then nothing here had any warmth left to it. The house was frozen, like her. Caught in a moment, a *dark* moment. Menacing.

Menace. That was exactly the feeling she got from the figure. It was flowing towards her in waves, threatening to swamp her. The lights continued to flicker as she hauled herself upwards, into further darkness, and yet…she was sure she'd left a landing light on. Trapped again. A caged animal. If only the lights downstairs would stop flickering! If only Jessica was more lucid! She'd ask her then, *demand* to know what had happened here, the joy that she'd tuned into, and then this…despair and rage.

*What happened to the children? What happened to him?*

"What did you do, Jessica?"

The figure, the shadow, whatever it was, broke completely free, whooshing between the light and the dark, coming for her, its mouth opening, and a roar escaping. A howl of pure anguish that the four walls complied with by amplifying.

She screamed too, bolting further up the stairs, to go… where? To her own room, or Jessica's? Jessica, who'd said after that terrible dream Isla had had, *I know.* Did she know about this too? Would she be sitting upright, fully awake, staring at her, mouthing those same words, then refusing to elaborate? Plaguing Isla with the mystery of it all, forcing imagining after imagining?

On the landing, she turned towards her room, and towards that other room at the far end. The door there – was it open, when it had been shut before? Such gloom upstairs! So difficult to see. Would someone be waiting in the doorway there as well, the same something which was behind her? A version of it?

She couldn't linger. There was no time. Which way to go? *Think, Isla! Think!* Was there safety anywhere in this house? Or would the shadows always find her?

"This way!"

It was a whisper in the air. She barely caught the words; only the urgency.

"Hurry!"

She spun around. The whisper was coming from the other side of the house.

"Hurry," it repeated.

Something at her back, something…cold, was reaching out. Fingers like tendrils of smoke, but no less dangerous because of it. *More* dangerous. Able to stop her heart if they touched her. Or burn her alive. And then she'd be truly trapped. Also a ghost. Something she didn't believe in. But no matter, because they existed despite that disbelief. In this house, even the living were shadows.

She ran, not towards Jessica's room or her own, but to the children's room – the door there standing open when, like the other, it had been closed before, and a light on. Music too – that of the figurine, although it was broken, wasn't it? She'd dropped and smashed it. Yet it was playing still, sweet notes slicing through the atmosphere.

"I'm coming," she yelled. To Amelia? To Gabriel? Was

it they who'd whispered to her, the giggling children, the *scampering* children? Dead, but only in body?

Whatever was behind her was close, almost upon her, and the children's room, down that long corridor, too far away. She'd never make it. She'd trip over her own feet, terror making her clumsy, then it'd be upon her, and would devour her indeed. She who had dared to enter its domain would now be paying the price for such folly.

Just a few more steps to go. Her body was faltering, slowing… Fear unable to override exhaustion. Where was Jessica in all this? Did she know, or was she dead already? While Isla had been downstairs getting drunk? *You've failed again, Isla!*

Perhaps she should succumb. She *deserved* all this. Such a wicked fate. No way to outrun it.

"NO!"

Something grasped her as the word was screamed out. Hands. Two sets of them. Rather than being dragged backwards into the arms of death, she was yanked towards the room at the far end, the nursery, the shrine. The door then slammed shut, those hands only letting go as she sank to the floor, sobs leaving her mouth, one after the other, unstoppable.

The music had stopped, though, and in here the atmosphere was calm. That sense of impending doom, of such danger, was – incredibly – dissipating.

She'd been pulled inside, and whatever was out there, *all* of it, banished.

Once again, she'd been saved.

# Chapter Eleven

## *24th December – Christmas Eve*

In the corner of the children's room, a lamp – that she *hadn't* turned on – cast the brightest of glows, softening the edges of the room, making it seem like she was dreaming again. But she was definitely awake, sitting up straight now, and gazing ahead. This was reality, but not like any reality she had ever known. The soft tick of a clock was the next thing that captured her attention, over there, on one of the shelves. Such busy shelves! Books stacked upon them, toy cars, china fairies, raggedy dolls that had slumped, and stiff-limbed teddy bears. All evidence that these children had been wanted and cherished. And in amongst their belongings, a clock, tick, tick, ticking away, causing her to rise at last, and make her way towards it.

Time had slipped. Something it did in this house, Isla also growing used to that. She reached out, her hand encircling the clock and bringing it closer. She was used to time slipping, but even so, how could this be? How could it *possibly* be? It was midnight already! Hours had passed since she'd built the second fire downstairs, and since she'd started drinking whisky. A whisky that was years old, vintage, that she'd drunk more of than intended. Was she drunk? Was all this, what she'd experienced since finding the bottle, not an imagining but a hallucination? There were drinks that could do that, such as Mescal, a tequila with a worm immersed in it. That worm, pickled though it was, could cause you to trip, as powerful as any drug. The drugs she used to like. That she'd taken regularly.

*Not now, Isla!*

No point in getting caught up in her own past; it was another's she was embroiled in here. She had to sober up, try to understand what was happening, and remember too that she was not the only living person in this house, as far as she knew. She couldn't stay in this room, but right now, she couldn't find it in herself to leave either.

Whoever had grabbed her hands and pulled her forwards, who'd helped her, were they still here somewhere? Hiding every bit as much as she was?

"Hello? Are you there? Thank you...thank you, for doing what you did, for helping me." Quickly glancing back at the door, she swallowed. "I don't know what that was coming after me, even if it was real. I just...What's going on here?"

A tinkling of laughter. Bright and hopeful, which she marvelled at. How could *anything* be hopeful in this place?

She scanned the room again. "Where are you? Let me see."

Carefully placing the clock back down, she backed up against the far wall, and slid down it, facing the entire room again, caught up in what was either a hallucination, a waking dream, or a reality bent completely out of shape. As she stared and stared, as she *willed* them into being, they obeyed. Two figures manifesting: a boy and a girl – the boy younger than the girl, as dark-haired as in the portrait, the girl as fair.

They were in the centre of the room, the boy pushing a wooden train along the rug, the girl clutching a doll in one hand and with the other pretending to brush its flaxen hair, seemingly unaware of Isla's presence. Just another replay. A scene that was all too fleeting, dissolving as another took its place. The same two children, this time chasing each other around the room, the boy with his head thrown back and laughing. They too faded, leaving behind mere wisps of themselves – and Isla wondering if they'd come back. She needed to see more, if she was ever to understand the mystery of Wildacre, and a situation she was at the mercy of.

There was a brief lull before the girl did indeed materialise, sitting up in bed, turning the pages of a picture book. Isla then looked over at the other bed, the one whose coverlet was blue. Sure enough, there was the boy, sleeping there, as angelic as his name suggested.

However strange these latest happenings were, Isla found herself relaxing into it. Such sweet scenes. Scenes that she'd imagined anyway, when she'd first come in here. She blinked when there appeared to be daylight, the children both awake and laughing, always laughing… Happy children. Content. She had nothing to fear from them. Still the brightness of day continued, and there was much activity in the room: a flurry of it, the children involved in…crayoning and painting, pieces of paper drawn on, coloured in, glittered, then folded. Decorations! That's what they were making, Isla's eyes strayed from them to the corner of the room by the window, where there was a small Christmas tree, its branches bare, however, waiting to be adorned.

They were young children. Surely there must be

someone helping them to craft such items. But peer as she might, the only two shapes Isla could see were Amelia and Gabriel. And yet…there was a sense of someone else in the room, as busy as the children, directing them, helping them. *Jessica?*

Yet another scene took the place of that one. All decorations had been made and were now being placed on the tree, Gabriel's hands eager, *too* eager, and being pulled back, but gently. Night fell once more in this other world, and there was a fire blazing in the grate. The two children were in bed again, but neither was asleep.

Such a lovely room, and such a cosy atmosphere. Maybe this was Christmas Eve, the night of, and that's why the children were awake, because they were so excited.

Isla smiled as she remembered feeling the same way. As she watched the children lying there, the pair of them fidgeting, tossing and turning, whispering to each other as flames glowed gently in the grate, as she felt the warmth of that fire easing at last the coldness in her bones, it seemed harmless to allow her mind to drift a little.

She had two brothers and a sister. Isla was the youngest, and yes, she had to admit, the most excitable. But her siblings would delight in seeing how she was on the run-up to Christmas. They would tease her too, pretending that Father Christmas wasn't coming if she'd misbehaved that day, or not done as she was told.

Her brow furrowed. Never mind about misbehaving. She wanted only the glory of Christmas, finding common ground with Amelia and Gabriel. But that thought, once in her mind, wouldn't fade. She was excitable…or another way to describe it: volatile. Prone to tantrums if she didn't get her way. Again, her family would laugh at this, and indulge her – mostly. There were times, though, when her tantrums, legendary or not, wouldn't be tolerated, when her brothers and sister would storm off, just so fed up with her, and her mother, usually so patient, would grow angry too.

"Stop that now, Isla!" she'd say, trying to make herself heard above the screams. "You're impossible, sometimes. Do you know that? Downright impossible."

Despite her behaviour, she was never overly punished. But the disappointment in her mother's face, her father's too when he got home and was told about what had happened, should have had more impact than it did.

Her father would come and talk to her.

"Now, Isla," he'd say, "tell me all about it. Why you're acting this way."

She'd been nine, way too old for tantrums, her mother would tell her. And yet, it was like there was something inside her that refused to dampen.

Her father was a kind man. He had dark hair threaded with grey, and his eyes crinkled around the edges when he smiled. Not that he was smiling during their chat. He'd had a long day. As an accountant he worked hard to support his family. Coming home and dealing with an errant daughter was probably the last thing he wanted.

She'd refused to speak to him. She'd turned her back, folded her arms and cried some more. He'd leant forwards and tried to hug her, but she'd pushed him off. Funny how the memory of that was so ripe, how *hard* she'd pushed him.

Later, she'd snuck to the top of the stairs to hear her mother and father talking. Her siblings were in their rooms, reading or listening to music on headphones.

"…the way she is."

"Spoilt."

"Not! Just…different…spirited."

"…fed up."

"I know…older…change."

"She'd better."

There'd then followed laughter between them, but with a fraught edge to it. Isla knew it was her they were talking about; her sister and brothers never gave as much trouble. That word, that description, *spirited*, followed her into her teenage years. The tantrums may have stopped, but that particular quality was only enhanced. Again, to the amusement of her family, more often than not. The life and soul of any party was what she aimed to be, because…she loved parties, loved events, loved any occasion where people came together. It was as though what was in her *soared* during those times. A show-off, hogging the limelight. Maybe. But it was just her way, '*Wouldn't be without her.*' She'd overheard her parents and siblings say that too, numerous times. The funny, cute, excitable surprise little sister, who grew and grew, whose behaviour suddenly became less endearing but more concerning instead.

She closed her eyes, although not before a tear squeezed through. Someone with as excitable a nature as hers needed nothing to heighten it, and yet there were so many things available that'd do exactly that. Stuff her friends were taking. *Fun* stuff.

Sensing movement in the room, a shift in atmosphere, she opened her eyes.

The children were in bed, but awake. That was the last scene there'd been. Excitable, too, Isla guessing it was Christmas Eve.

The children were *still* awake, still in bed, but the girl was sitting upright now and doing that thing Jessica did, clutching at the front of her nightdress, her eyes wide as she stared at the door. The boy was half-sitting, half-slouching, his eyes also wide and trained on the door, expecting what? Someone to burst through it? Not Father Christmas. This was someone they weren't so eager to see.

Her own memories faded, to be replaced again by theirs, Amelia and Gabriel's. She also turned her head to the door, as fearful as she had been before. What if that thing that had chased her wasn't gone, was still out there, making itself taller, wider, determined to batter the door down if it had to?

Her hands on the floor, she scrabbled away from it, shaking, cold again, like ice. *This place! What is this place?* Not dreamy or romantic, but cursed.

"Oh God, oh God, oh God," she heard herself muttering, as the little boy climbed out of bed and ran barefooted over to his sister. Amelia reached out for him, dragging him into bed with her. The pair of them huddled, as she'd seen them do twice before: at the top of the stairs, and in her bedroom.

Gabriel was crying. Amelia looked as if she was trying to be stronger. Her cheeks were dry, but she was shaking as she braced herself.

"Who is it?" Isla begged. "Who's out there?"

If they heard her, these wisps, these shards of memory, they gave no sign.

There was a bang on the door, just as there'd been a bang on that other door, at the opposite end of the house, someone desperate to enter. Was the door locked? Her eyes travelled to just below the handle. There seemed to be a key poking out of it. Who had locks on bedroom doors in their own homes? Home was a safe haven, or was supposed to be.

Somewhere you could escape from danger, not run headlong into it.

The little girl was crying now, her bravery diminishing.

"It's okay," Isla said, hoping that somehow she'd be able to hear her, "you *are* brave. You are. Look at what you're doing, trying to protect your little brother, to comfort him. But what from, Amelia? What's going to happen?"

The banging stopped, to be replaced by another roar, this one filled with utter frustration. Another voice joined the mêlée, higher-pitched and screaming at the other, the deeper voice soon retaliating. A torrent of words were exchanged, although Isla couldn't make sense of them, only that they were saturated with a rage as explosive as dynamite. The harder she listened, the more muffled the voices became. Had they moved away, the two outside? Taken their argument elsewhere?

*Not in front of the children!* That's what her mother used to say, should she and Isla's father have cross words. As if children were sacred, and couldn't possibly be exposed to such things, their world kept perfect. Something Isla found she was both grateful for and angry about. Lives weren't perfect. People weren't. So why pretend? Put that pressure on yourselves and others to toe an impossible line, to be something you're not. Also, to feel terrible about mistakes made, so terrible you'd do… what? Run away? Disappear? To disappear was exactly what these children were trying to do now, squashed against Amelia's headboard, as if hoping it would somehow envelop them. Another portal, taking them anywhere but here.

"It's okay," she whispered to them. "They're gone. And I think the door's locked."

Rising, she made her way over to them, wished she could

reach out and stroke their hair, the girl's a silky yellow, and the dark curls of the boy. Lavished with gifts, but they also knew fear. It was clear they were bewildered by it. Confused. There'd been happy times in this house. Jessica had described them. Isla had *seen* them, but there'd been this too: the tempest, as Jessica herself had described it.

She knelt by the bed, looking up at them. Insubstantial they might be, but earlier she'd felt them, when they'd taken her by the hand and pulled her into this room.

"Take my hand again," she urged. "Listen to me. Look at me. It's okay now. What happened, is over. You don't have to keep reliving it."

Was it her imagination, or had the little girl tensed further, her eyes flickering to the left, to where Isla knelt? Her head turned a fraction too.

Isla breathed deeply with wonder. "You can hear me? You know I'm here?"

If so, she was meant to see their story unfolding. All of it. But why?

"Amelia! Gabriel! You know I'm here, don't you? And it's okay, you're safe now."

Amelia's face contorted in horror. At the same time, Gabriel's eyes closed as he tucked himself further under his sister's arm. There was something else too: a slam as the door flew open, either unlocked, or the lock unable to withstand the force of what was now in the room with them, that they'd only found temporary refuge from.

It was advancing, almost leisurely now, arrogantly confident that its quarry could find no further harbour, that they were completely at its command. Helpless.

Two children. On Christmas Eve.

Isla wanted to turn, to shout at whatever it was behind

them. '*You bastard! You coward. How could you frighten them like this?*' But the words remained solely in her head; her eyes on the children, and only them.

The girl *knew* she was there! Dragging her eyes from the entity, she turned her head further in Isla's direction, all the way, until their gaze met.

Isla, unable to breathe, could only project her thoughts. *What do I do?*

The answer came, just before the children vanished – as did the fire in the grate that had become frenzied – and, thankfully, the presence that loomed over them all.

"Help." The voice was childish indeed. "You should help."

# Chapter Twelve

## *24<sup>th</sup> December – Christmas Eve*

Fragments of daylight entering the room caused Isla's eyelids to flutter, at last opening to see where she was: the children's bedroom, at the far end of the house.

She was lying on Amelia's bed, although couldn't remember having climbed onto it, or at what point sleep had claimed her. Pushing herself upwards, she winced. Her head thumped, courtesy of the whisky she'd drunk last night. *Only because of that?*

It took probably a further minute to remember what else had happened during the evening hours. Just snatches of it came back at first, initially making her smile. How she'd danced in the hallway, imagining herself to be a young Jessica. *A woman in love.* That was it. Helplessly in love. *Obsessed.*

Then, in a rush, all that happened returned, the magical *and* the macabre: the lights that had flickered and wouldn't stop, something breaking free of the shadows, a figure that had chased her, full of wrath. The children! They'd saved her, bringing her into this room, their domain, their world – which was also magical at first, until something rotten had reared up and smashed it, all those years ago, in 1960.

Amelia had turned her head towards Isla, and begged for

help. Isla swallowed as she recalled that too, her skin flushing both hot and cold. How could you help ghosts? Stop what had already transpired? A tragedy. An accident or…murder. *Amelia, Gabriel, were you murdered?*

There was no reply, no sense of anything other than the weight of emptiness.

She had no way of knowing. Unless…

Shuffling forwards, she swung both legs onto the floor. *Unless what, Isla?* Unless Jessica told her, of course. Unless Jessica remembered.

Jessica was lucid, sometimes, coherent. Could Isla get her to be that way again?

Rising, she glanced over at the Christmas tree, at the handmade decorations that the children had helped to make: the paper chains, the colours of them so faded, pink when they should be red, the yellow bleached to white. Beyond the tree, she could see the rain was back. The sun didn't shine here, not any more. But sixty years was a long time to be in the dark, to have lived as Jessica had, as a recluse, venturing out only for essentials, but lately, not even that. If she'd had a car, she didn't any longer. It was a long, long time to live with memories but also to run *from* them, shutting up rooms where lives had been lived, *their* lives, disposing of anything personal, any reminders. And yet this room, the children's… It would have been a bridge too far to have touched anything there.

A tragedy could alter you. Isla knew that all too well, but could it also drive you insane? Is that was she was dealing with here: insanity? Not just Jessica's, but someone else's too? That other being who was still here, haunting Wildacre, as Amelia and Gabriel were? *You're dead. Three of you. And yet you still remain.*

Jessica was her charge. Her…responsibility. A woman who was also haunting this place, also unable to leave. Who Isla had to go to, right now, wondering again as she moved forwards, could it be that she'd died too? Finally?

How quiet the house was this Christmas Eve morning. Even the rain outside was falling gently. Calm. That's how she'd describe the atmosphere. But a strange calm. As if someone had taken the deepest of breaths and was waiting to exhale.

She continued down the corridor, past the staircase, briefly looking downwards, noting no lights flickering in the hallway. Not any more. Peaceful. For now. During daylight hours. But night followed day – and in December, all too quickly.

Perhaps she could dress the old woman warmly, and they could both leave. Her car was useless, but they could still head to it, and she could place Jessica into the back seat and lock the doors, then continue alone on foot. And her cough, her fever, didn't feel so bad this morning, she was numb again, which was preferable.

Another plan. A good one. Jessica was as light as a bird. Isla could practically carry her if need be, the prospect of escape something she was desperate for, to turn and run, as that other carer had – but unlike them, with Jessica in tow. A dying woman.

A woman who had stayed at Wildacre despite everything, because her children were there. The memory of them, their graves, their very souls even. If Isla tried to make her leave, would she fight against it? Her agony only increasing?

And then there were the children themselves. Amelia and Gabriel who had helped her, and then begged her to do the same for them. To leave them at Wildacre, without Jessica, with only that other, who bayed for blood… Could she do it? To save her own soul? A soul that would then be truly damned?

Outside Jessica's door, Isla paused, looking only briefly in the direction of that other room further down the corridor, where something else had taken place. More horror. For that's what the atmosphere was spliced with: horror.

And the key to it all was Jessica. She had the answers to everything.

Entering the room, Isla saw that Jessica was sleeping on her back, and breathing evenly. Or rather…she was *pretending* to sleep, because Isla had caught it: the woman's head turning quickly, from the direction of the door to straight ahead; the eyes that had been open, suddenly closing.

No more hesitation. Isla walked straight up to the bed, saw the glass of water untouched by the bedside, and smelt what was in the air. Something as sickly-sweet as the tinned fruit. The smell of death, she supposed, fast approaching.

"Not yet, though," she whispered, bending so that Jessica could clearly hear her words. "The time to die is not yet, not when there's something that needs to be resolved. Jessica," she said, her voice growing louder, "you have to tell me what happened. I know you know, you've told me that. But now I want to know too."

\* \* \*

Unresponsive. No matter what Isla did, Jessica would not even see her, let alone talk to her. Her eyes remained averted the whole time, and she mumbled to herself a fresh set of unintelligible words. Having entered her room earlier, Isla had left again, going downstairs to get some tea and eat some tinned fruit. Her nose wrinkled as she chased cubed peaches and pears around the dish, resolving that in future she'd stick only to the fresh stuff. She also craved some fresh bread, one of those fancy sourdough loaves, and some fresh butter to spread on it. A treat. At Christmas. That's what it'd be like. But in this house, there'd been no homage paid to the festive season at all. Not for a long time. Years and years. Sheets thrown over everything.

*Isla, there are drawers and cupboards galore in this house – you've opened just a few of them.* That was right, she had. She was paid to help, not pry. Some carers snooped, she knew that. If she saw them at the agency and had a cup of tea with them between jobs, they'd talk about the jewellery they'd sifted through at their clients' houses, the owners oblivious. They'd never taken anything, they'd been at pains to point out, but Isla wasn't so sure. A fair few clients couldn't even remember their own names, let alone what they possessed, so it would be an easy steal. Isla would sit and listen, and despise them for it, the callousness with which they'd talked, the detachment. And so no, she didn't pry. A client's private life belonged to them, just as her own life belonged to her. If anyone should delve further into her life, she'd be horrified. *You'd be ashamed too, Isla, don't forget that.*

She shook her head to rid it of such thoughts. She respected her clients, but here, at Wildacre, Jessica Lockhart's past had sought Isla out, and forced her to take notice. *Because of the children? Because you have to save them as well as Jessica?*

If it was Jessica who had stripped this place, what a job she'd made of it. All but one room was absent of personality, of any clues. Isla could see it in her mind's eye. The fire she could have built in the grounds, such…private grounds, hurling onto it everything to do with her past, every reminder that was simply too painful to be confronted with over and over again. Then retiring to her room, almost as barren as the rest of the house, to live her half-life. Christmas Eve. That was the day it happened. Whatever 'it' was.

The liquid in her mug of tea sloshed over the rim slightly as she held it. She placed it down and gripped the edges of the counter to steady herself.

The day it happened… The day that…death happened, of course. A supposedly joyous day, but the very opposite. The anniversary. Jessica's *last* Christmas, as it was unlikely she'd see another, even if Isla could get her any medical help.

If she didn't solve this mystery, and save Amelia and Gabriel as Amelia had asked her to, she wondered again if Jessica would become like them, and trapped here? Her body removed, but not the essence of her, her spirit. All would be caught in an endless loop of fear that just kept replaying within Wildacre.

Nonsense. All of it. Too far-fetched. Back at the agency, if she were listening to someone relate a story like this, telling it like they believed it, she'd think them batshit crazy. But out here, in the rain-soaked countryside, in a house where the past persisted despite its owner trying to eradicate it, in such splendid *isolation*, she could believe all too well what was happening. And despite this, she wouldn't run, not unless she had to. She'd see it through. How to offer Jessica or the children any kind of redemption, she had no idea, but if there was a way, she had to find it.

She turned her back on the tea, no longer seeking solace from the warmth of it, for there was none to be had. Not yet. There were indeed still drawers and cupboards to open and close, to search through, but one room in particular she felt she must go to first. The room at the far end of her corridor, that footsteps had hurried to once upon a time, that the roar had emanated from. A room that the past was trying to lead her to, she realised, but which oozed so much dread and terror.

Never more so than now.

She didn't want to go to that room. She continued to stand there, in a kitchen that even if she had industrial-strength products to hand would never gleam. Not now.

*But once it had.* She could almost smell the aroma of baking in the air, the spices that had been used to create both savoury and sweet dishes, Christmas cake, perhaps. Christmas pudding. Mince pies – dozens of them. A smell that wouldn't linger, although she willed it to. The familiar stench of decay replaced it.

A house that was lost. Children that were lost too. The devil after them?

Those graves outside, two that were named, and one that wasn't – was the latter where the devil resided? Whatever he'd done, Jessica couldn't let go of him either, not entirely, and had therefore put them all at peril. Graves that were choked by ivy, as so much at Wildacre was, not tended to in years. No evidence whatsoever of any posy left there, no withered stems or petals that had since crumbled to confetti. If he was indeed the devil, what was it that kept her so tightly bound to him? She shook her head. What a conundrum Jessica Lockhart was! Rejecting and clinging to the past in equal measure. If she had ever wandered to the graves, reached out and touched the cold, cold stone, almost caressing it, had her gaze then shifted to the mound, her eyes narrowing, wishing the ivy would choke it further, that wish not relieving her pain but increasing it.

About to leave the kitchen, having taken several strides, she stopped just short of entering the corridor which would lead her to the hallway and the staircase there.

*It wasn't just their names written on Amelia and Gabriel's headstones, remember?*

What else was there? She struggled to recall, and later would wonder at this, why she'd disregarded the most vital information of all.

*I Have Risen!*

Christmas Eve. The morning of. But daylight would only last for so long.

An anniversary rising up fast to meet her. The ghosts of the past doing the same.

She burst from the kitchen, her heart keeping pace with the pounding of her feet.

# Chapter Thirteen

## 24<sup>th</sup> December – Christmas Eve

Would she have run as fast if night had indeed fallen? Strange how the light made you braver, more determined, even if that light was half-hearted.

At the top of the stairs, Isla emerged onto the landing, half-daring whatever had chased her up there the previous evening to try again, when she wasn't so frightened, when she'd dug and dug and found purpose. *I Have Risen!* The children were here, inside the house. Not outside. Little wonder, then, that Jessica rarely if ever visited their burial site. Heaven was a place you were supposed to go to after death, if you'd lived a good life, that is. And children *would* live a good life, too young to succumb to wicked ways. Even she, Isla, had been good when a kid. Prone to tantrums, admitted, even petulant on occasion, a show-off, an attention-seeker. But in a kid you can forgive those things, because they were learning. Reach a certain age, though, and you were supposed to change. She had changed, for the worse. Grown-up, but only in body. Amelia and Gabriel never had a chance to grow. And now they were stuck at Wildacre, haunting it. Ghosts indeed. A place that had once been like heaven, but was now the very opposite.

There was no one in pursuit of her, and only the sound

of her own feet as she thundered past Jessica's room, and her own, past other rooms – unused, bereft of everything, even secrets. Only the far room held a secret. *His* room? The devil?

On reaching the door to that room, she grabbed the handle and pushed at it. There was no resistance. It opened as willingly as the children's room had, as if…welcoming her. Imagination? Or instinct? *Everyone* wanted resolve here.

A room as musty as the others, there was a bed in it, the brown coverlet mildewed. In fact, there was mildew everywhere, more so than when she'd stood in the doorway before and looked in. She was sure of it. Like contagion, it had spread.

With blackened spores in every corner, it was a room that was not fit for purpose, in a house that wasn't. A house that had lived with fear and sorrow for too long, and was now buckling under the pressure. Finally. On Christmas Eve.

Her nose wrinkling at the smell of the mould, sourer than in any other room, she hurried over to a chest positioned by the window. Before opening any drawers, she glanced outwards. As from Jessica's room, you could see the gravestones of the children from there. If this was his room, Jessica's husband, the children's father, would he do as she was doing now, and stare at them? Was he…responsible for their deaths? A reign of tyranny? For only a tyrant would roar that way, surely, trying everything they could to inspire terror in their victims. And then he'd died himself.

"Bastard," she breathed, something she'd called him before, but not here, in what was as much an epicentre as the children's room. Was he lurking just behind her, out of sight for now, in what shadow there was, but becoming more substantial as daylight faded? Something dead, but which had life in them nonetheless?

Her attention back on the chest, she hauled the drawers open, one by one, doing as she'd done in the study, running her hands over each panel, searching, searching, searching, her hands coming away empty.

"What did you do with his things, Jessica? With everything?" Her voice, filled with frustration, was a roar as well. "Did you do what I think you did? Take it outside and burn it? Or stow it away in the attic? You can't get rid of the past like that!" Raising a hand, she thumped at her chest. "You can't, because it lives here, inside us. I know because I've tried to erase it too, but it makes no difference. It doesn't shift."

A sob caught in her throat, and her eyes watered. She sniffed hard, blinked rapidly and swallowed her own sorrow, not wanting to add to the load.

She swung around. This *was* his room. His personal space. Some people did that, didn't they, in the past, in these big fancy houses? They'd 'visit' each other if wanting certain needs to be met, then return to their own room. And he *was* still here, the head of the family, the mould creeping further, she swore it, and just so, so black.

Almost hurling herself at the bed, she tore the coverlet and sheets from it, imagining the spores that covered it rising into the air, mingling with the dust, making her cough. Hunkering down as she retched violently.

*You're what's making me ill. Wildacre. All that festers inside you.*

It had nothing to do with getting drenched in the rain when she'd first come here. Was it only three days ago? It seemed so much longer, as if she'd been here for decades too, a fly entangled in the web that had been woven.

Finally, the retching eased, and she could stand again, the bedding at her feet giving her a sense of triumph. *There's nowhere to hide, not any more.*

The room also contained an in-built wardrobe, a dull pale *splintering* wood running the entire length of the far wall.

As her gaze swept the length and breadth of it, her skin tingled. It was as though someone had reached out and touched her from behind, as before, not one pair of hands but two, pushing her forwards gently. Or tentatively. It was hard to tell.

She took a step forward, but only one as another thought occurred. *Is it me bringing you back to life, Amelia and Gabriel? And the man I imagined to be your father, tall, dark and handsome – beguiling – but also the devil? What if Jessica didn't have a husband or a lover? What if the mound is merely that? Am I creating all this?*

But what had happened downstairs, when she'd been whisky-soaked, the arms that had wrapped themselves around her, the feelings that had been so intense… How could she imagine a love so profound, so deep, so…all-consuming, when actually love like that was still a mystery to her? Somehow, she'd stepped into Jessica's shoes. Those were her feelings, and nothing to do with Isla.

*We're all orphans of the storm.* An *eternal* storm. But who were the orphans exactly, the stranded, the abandoned? The vulnerable?

The children at her back were growing impatient.

She must go to the wardrobe. Something was inside it. Something…telling.

Never had she been so curious. Never had she also wanted to run as fast as she could, away from there. What should she do for the best? Unearth this further? Push it to the limits? What would happen then? What would she encounter next?

Those fingers were jabbing at her now. *Go on! Go on!* Their voices were echoing around her head, in perfect harmony with each other.

Who should she trust here? Could she even trust herself?

There was insanity at Wildacre. Minds that had slipped, that had broken.

Jessica could not be considered sane, not any more. But was old age really the reason? And what if madness spread like the mould in this room, the very thing to have got inside Isla? Jessica would end her days here, but again she feared that she would too. If only she could run. But she couldn't even turn, because if she did, she'd see those children. Not as they were in their bedroom, but as something broken too.

More steps forward, the silence oppressive. That sense of expectation too, of someone holding their breath. Soon they'd exhale, the storm erupting all over again.

All too soon she reached the wardrobe. All too soon she'd learn something that she both did and didn't want to know, but which was now inevitable.

It seemed – no matter how absurd – that all avenues in her life, all roads she'd taken, had led her to this point, to intervene in the lives of others, strangers, to help them. And yet all she'd ever thought about before Wildacre was herself. But she was changing, no longer running, had *chosen* to stay. To see events through. All in the name of atonement. Because without it…what was there?

Life had been so lonely. Even outside this place, she'd been a shadow. When she looked in the mirror, she didn't recognise herself, seeing the same bleakness that existed in abundance within these four walls. Twenty-four, that's all she was. She'd lived this way for two years. Two years too long. An orphan herself. She'd made it that way. Every bit as lonely as Jessica. But Jessica had endured. For years and years and years she'd endured, retreating further from the world.

Could she, Isla, do it for as long? Stay here, even, at Wildacre, after Jessica had died, hoping no one would come for her, that she could forget…and be forgotten?

*Do you really want to forget?*

Because Jessica hadn't. The shrine was proof of that.

*What happened here? What happened in my own life? What do I have to do to make everything better?*

The answer was but a whisper: *Open the wardrobe door.*

A door that slid sideways on castors, her hand inching it back. So much was empty here, but this wasn't. Immediately she saw it. An outline of something. Portrait-shaped, a frame around it, golden, ornate, fussy. What lay within the frame was concealed completely by darkness. It had to be pulled into the light. *Liberated.*

She didn't want to touch it, imagining mould to have infected it too, but she reached out nonetheless, and grasped it.

It was something else Jessica couldn't quite let go of. Another memory. The missing portrait. The one that Isla had wondered about, that used to hang in the hallway between Amelia and Gabriel's portraits. Not a family portrait. It was of two people, a man and a woman, but every bit as romantically captured.

With something like wonder, she hauled it further over to the window so she could see it better, having to kick the bedclothes out of the way.

Jessica… she was as beautiful as Isla had suspected. Fair hair so like Amelia's, framing a heart-shaped face, and eyes (as blue as her daughter's) that sought out Isla's gaze, eager to convey she was happy, content, full of love. *Overly* eager?

She was wearing a simple patterned dress. Pink and violet flowers against a pale background. The skirt fell almost to her ankles, seeming like a mark of her innocence, her purity. Of renewal, even, rendering life before this man meaningless. It was a dress you might expect a Jane Austen heroine to wear, that Isla had seen in films, with a pretty lace edging around the neckline. She was leaning into the man, their hands entwined, giving herself entirely to him. Body and soul.

Behind them, hills stretched into the distance. The sky was greeny-blue, the sun lending a golden glow. It was too romantic for the age they'd lived in. Delusional, even?

Having been fixated on Jessica, Isla's gaze fell on the man, wanted to see if the same depth of love on Jessica's face was on his – returned, wholeheartedly.

He was wearing a long evening jacket and black pleated trousers, smart shoes peeking out from beneath them. His stance…a little stiff, perhaps? More uncomfortable than Jessica's. That was all she could glean, though. It was impossible to tell any more. Impossible because his face had been slashed at, with the sharpest of knives. Hacked at, again and again, until totally destroyed.

It wasn't a roar that finally caused her to turn around, although she expected to hear it, there in her ear, a shadow having crept close to her. It wasn't the scampering of feet either; the children running away, both excited and frightened by this discovery, by what it could unleash. It was merely the softest of sighs.

She turned. There was Jessica, filling the doorway, standing in her nightdress, but not clutching at the front of it this time. Her hands were hanging loosely by her side as her eyes travelled from Isla's face to the painting.

There was defiance in them, Isla noticed. A hardness that offset how rheumy they were, making her look more alive. Not such a shadow.

Jessica opened her mouth to speak, but Isla knew what she'd say.

"Now you know," she uttered, quickly repeating herself. "Now you know."

# Chapter Fourteen

## *24<sup>th</sup> December – Christmas Eve*

The silence at Wildacre, when it existed, was something tangible. You felt you could reach out and grab it, wring the life from it, end it, because it was just so deafening. Isla wanted to answer Jessica back, to say, "Know what?" but the silence endured, with Jessica about-turning and walking back down the corridor to her own room.

Isla stayed where she was, her mind in turmoil. Know what? she asked herself that question at least. That this man existed? That you loved him, once? That he's dead too, because he is, isn't he, Jessica? That isn't just a mound out there, as sometimes I've tried to convince myself. It's his grave. He's at Wildacre, alongside the two children. Your children, Jessica, and his. Did he die in 1960 too? On the same day? How? Who was responsible? She had so many questions, but it wasn't her who could provide the answers. Finally, she turned back to the portrait, to the area where the canvas had been brutally ruined. By Jessica's hand? Who else's?

She needed facts, not more imaginings. Without them, there'd be no peace for anyone. Not on earth or in the heavens.

When Jessica was in the doorway, she'd been perfectly

lucid. Perhaps, if Isla acted fast, that clarity would remain.

She moved so quickly that she felt a rush of feverish giddiness, with waves of hot and cold engulfing her. Stopping, and after a few deep breaths, she tried again, hurtling into the corridor, and down the length of it, all the way to Jessica's room.

"Jessica," she said, on entering. "Jessica, listen to me! What happened here, all those years ago? What did you do?"

She was in bed, sheets and blankets covering her. Mute.

"Oh no, no you don't." Isla rushed up to her. "I know you can hear me. I know you're perfectly capable at times, that you can walk, you can talk, and you can remember. Jessica," she continued, wanting to grab the woman, to shake her, no matter how thin she was, and make her listen, "your children, Amelia and Gabriel, are dead, but they're here. And him, your husband, your lover, whoever he was, is here too. Everyone is frightened, angry, and confused. You haven't let go of the past. You've kept it alive, Jessica, not me. I'm not responsible. Only you. Those epitaphs on the children's graves, those words. I Have Risen! Did you force them to do that, and him too? Why, Jessica? Because of guilt? What do you have to be guilty about?"

An onslaught of words, a torrent of them, tripping over each other in their haste to be heard. Footsteps, outside Jessica's room, interrupted her. The echo of something, laughter quickly turning into urgent whisperings. Be quiet! Be quiet! Don't let them hear us, any of them. Is that what they were saying, Amelia begging Gabriel?

Isla had thought she'd go mad if she stayed here any longer, but perhaps it was already too late for that. This was a maddening place, with Jessica ensuring that year on year the divide between the material and the spiritual world eroded.

"Get up, Jessica," Isla commanded. "Get up and come with me."

The woman whimpered, shaking her head.

"Yes, Jessica! Face up to what happened here. You'll never rest until you do, okay? Not even after you've taken your last breath. I stayed here, I decided I'd help, I was begged to help. And I don't think I'll be able to leave either if I fail to do that. Fail…again." She took a deep breath, her chest heaving. "I won't fail! Not this time. There's terror here, but also such sorrow…" her eyes filled with tears as the truth of it hit her. "It'll become my sorrow, Jessica, and…and I won't be able to bear it. I've enough of my own to deal with." As there came more footsteps from the corridor, someone indeed running, she finally laid hands on the woman and lifted her. "When you've seen, you can't unsee. That's the trouble. When you know, you can't unknow."

Jessica didn't fight her. There were no hands flailing, trying to cling to the sheets and stay where she was. Perhaps she simply didn't have the strength left any more. Perhaps she knew as Isla did: time was running out.

With Jessica on her feet now, still murmuring to herself, her head hanging low, Isla traipsed them both forwards. Again, from afar, there came whisperings, creaks and groans from the house, as if it was shifting itself and waking more fully.

In the corridor, she steered the woman to the left. Their backs were to the room with the ruined portrait. Still Jessica was whimpering, a sound that was simply part of the rhythm here, that had been forged over the decades.

Whatever had happened, whatever Jessica's part in it,

there was no doubt she'd suffered since. Isla kept that at the forefront of her mind as they continued towards the staircase, then past it. A flickering of lights from below caught the corner of her eye, but she ignored it, determined that nothing would stop them from reaching their destination – not even the stairs creaking as though someone were on them.

"Come on," she urged the old woman, "we have to hurry."

There it was: the children's room, at the end of the corridor. Her clutch on Jessica tightening, she was aware the landing lights had also begun to flicker.

"Jessica, quickly. Just a bit further."

She could wait no more. A few steps in front of the room, Isla extended a leg and kicked at the door, expecting it to fly open. She was surprised when it didn't.

No, she thought, you don't get to resist, not now we've come this far. Gritting her teeth, she kicked again and again. "Bloody open, will you? You have to!"

Another creak, but not on the stairs, it was much closer than that, behind her. A wave of anger that rushed towards them, as thick as molasses.

A dream. A feverish life. Reality. All had merged into one here, as frayed at the edges as the runner beneath her feet. The light and the darkness, the house was full of both. But in the room she was trying to get into, that's where memories were at their strongest. A room which would jog memory, taking both Isla and Jessica back to a better – and a worse – time. A gift that was snatched from Wildacre, at a time when gifts were received. The truth buried as deep as the children's bodies.

"Fucking open," she screamed, feeling whatever was at

her back falter. Her own anger, bitterness, and misplaced resentment, all of which had brewed for far too long, now in competition with it. "Whatever this is, it's over," she continued, her voice shaking, but no longer with fear. "It ends tonight. Tomorrow is Christmas Day. It is not a day for darkness. Love and hope will live again, in all our souls. Yours and mine, Jessica, in Amelia and Gabriel's too, and even in yours, whoever it is that stalks us. So just open the door, and have the fucking courage to face this."

She put her entire might behind another kick, but the door flew open before her foot even touched it.

It was a triumph that bolstered her, but that also caused fear to return, because dealing with the truth, it was never easy.

They entered the room, Isla quickly closing the door and turning the key. The rain at the windows such a hard rain.

Isla chose Amelia's bed to sit her down on. The old woman, still with her head bent, was refusing to look around. Isla feared something else too: that she wouldn't resurface, that this was all in vain.

She knelt in front of her and took her hands, noting the coldness of them. She heard a keening from someone in the corridor, but inside the room all was quiet. The children, if they were there, were patiently waiting.

"Jessica," she said, "it's okay, it's all right. You can tell me anything. I won't judge."

The woman lifted her head a fraction, then whispered one word that Isla only just caught. "Anything?"

"Yes! If you're the guilty one, you can tell me. If you're…the murderer."

A gasp from the woman, her body flinching.

Isla held firm.

131

"Like I said, I won't judge, I'm in no position to. Because I'm a murderer too."

# Chapter Fifteen

## *24<sup>th</sup> December – Christmas Eve*

The floodgates had opened. The water was rushing through.

At Isla's words, Jessica lifted her head more fully and stared into Isla's eyes, clutched at her hands even harder. "Let me tell you this," she said, "before there was murder, there was love in this house! Our cup overflowed. It was *filled* with love."

She'd then turned her head in the direction of the window, to what was in front of it: the Christmas tree of course, with the decorations she'd helped her children make, an annual task set to become tradition, not just to decorate the small tree but several, one in the living room and one in the hallway, Isla able to imagine perfectly well how much they would have glittered. Nothing here was done by halves.

After several moments, and with her gaze back on Isla, Jessica described a time before children, when she'd been alone at Wildacre, as she was now, living not with real people, but with other ghosts: those of her parents.

"An orphan, that's what I became. Nineteen and alone. An heiress. This…" letting go of Isla's hands, she made a sweeping movement, "…was what I inherited, a house so large I'd rattle around it. A family house, the house in which I was born, *my house*, do you hear? My world. My security.

Their gift to me. Tell me, why does everything happen at Christmas in this house? Both the good and the bad. Because that's when they died, my mother and father, so suddenly, during the Christmas holidays. They'd left me, only for a short while, gone into Jedburgh shopping, but never made it back. There was a car crash. A collision. They died instantly. The shock tore me in two, cracked my heart, sent me spiralling into loneliness."

"Jessica, I'm so sorry—" Isla began, but Jessica pushed herself upwards and moved closer to the Christmas tree, half-reaching out as if to touch it, but then seemingly thought better of it, as though wondering, like Isla, if perhaps it would crumble beneath her fingertips. Not something that was real at all, but an illusion.

"I haven't been in this room for years," she breathed.

"You kept it exactly like it was," Isla responded.

"Yes. Yes, I did. How could I not?"

"Jessica—"

The old woman turned around, her eyes with the same misty quality the portraits contained.

"After my parents' deaths, I lived here alone, hugging the memory of them to myself, shunning the living. But then…" a smile tugged at her lips "…I always tended to do that. I wasn't like my parents, who'd sometimes venture out, meet people, mingle. I much preferred to tuck myself away. I loved it when it was just the three of us, when my world was that small. They'd talk about me, my parents, I'd hear them. Different, they called me, wondering if I'd change as I grew older. I don't think they minded the way I was, though, not really. They *indulged* me. Always. We were a unit. Inseparable. Until fate intervened, that is." She paused, then sighed a little. "Fate is so unkind, but sometimes, just sometimes, it can wear the sweetest face."

Jessica swayed. Isla was alarmed at first, fearing she was having some kind of attack, that her legs would give way and she'd collapse and die there and then, leaving the story cruelly unfinished. But that hint of a smile she wore widened. She was dancing, Isla realised, actually dancing! Those very same movements reminding her of the way she herself had danced in the hallway below, in another's arms, someone who had held her so tight, so close.

Not just watching Jessica, not just listening to her, it was as though Isla was *becoming* her, hypnotised by her swaying movements.

*We're one,* she thought as she closed her eyes, as she took Jessica's place on Amelia's bed. *Kindred spirits who've found each other.* Was that music she could also hear, accompanying Jessica's words? Not from the figurine, rather it was the same rhythm she'd heard downstairs, as soothing as a lullaby sung to a child.

*So alike,* was her final conscious thought. *Both seeking mercy.*

\* \* \*

As much as someone might want to shun the world, you couldn't, not entirely. Now that she was on her own and there was no one to carry out essential tasks for her, she had no choice but to undertake them herself.

Sheltered… She supposed she always had been. Something her mother would joke about. "Too fey for this world. Too…delicate." Her father agreed. Was it wrong to be like that? They didn't seem to think so – or if they did, they never let on. 'Out of time, and out of place.' They'd said that about her too, but that was incorrect, for she had this place, Wildacre, where she belonged.

Gregarious people, her parents, on occasions. They liked to entertain and invite others into their home, but it was different for her. She did not. They were honest with each other, always, and so she was honest about her dislike of it. The dinner parties, the gatherings, the events, gradually became fewer and fewer.

But she was growing, and didn't need attention every minute of every day. She could be left alone, which again she didn't mind. She would read, or bake, or tend to the gardens. There was plenty to keep her busy. And so they socialised elsewhere.

Sometimes she wondered, did she force them to do that? And therefore, no matter how unwittingly, cause their deaths? Was she to blame for everything?

When the news came… Oh, the howl that had left her lips! The grief, the anguish that followed. She couldn't think of it. She wouldn't. She'd stay where she was, in the house that was now hers and hers alone, and keep the memory of them alive: remembering how they were. The smiles, and the laughter, their presence in every room, in the study, in the library, her father smoking his pipe whilst reading the papers, her mother sometimes knitting, or listening to a play on the radio.

She'd hear them, in the quiet reaches of the night. Echoes of conversation that drifted upwards. And she'd smile, bringing the coverlet closer and urging them all the while: *Keep talking. Stay. You belong here too.* But over time, and despite her best efforts, their voices faded, until there was only silence.

Despair would overwhelm her. She'd sit in the living

room, surrounded by all the things they'd collected on their journey through life, and she'd cry. The black marble fireplace, once a favourite gathering place, was dark and silent too.

She grew thin. Lines appeared around her eyes, lines that shouldn't be there on skin as young as hers. For a long while, she didn't care. Maybe…if she stopped eating, stopped drinking, she could join them too. They'd be reunited.

*Where are you? Here or there? I can't hear you any more. I want to hear you!*

Surely, they wouldn't leave her, their only child. They'd doted on her.

She was an orphan. No longer did she have a family. Only memories.

In the end, it was hunger that drove her out, and the possibility that they were indeed still with her, just hiding, and therefore no need to go to such drastic lengths to join them. Several times she'd gone into Jedburgh – her parents had bought her a car when they were alive, encouraging her to drive it, although she never really had. With shaking hands, she'd navigate thankfully empty roads, gradually gaining confidence, heading to the grocers, the butcher, the baker, and to a café where she would sit with a cup of tea, and stare out of the window, thinking her parents might walk by, arm in arm. Always like that, conjoined, two people who'd lived – and died – together, but were also a part of her. She imagined how their heads would turn to see her sitting there, that familiar smile on her father's face as he lifted his hand to wave. *Hurry home,* he'd mouth. *We'll see you there.*

Tears fell on her cheeks. Always, she'd sit there crying, with those around her pretending not to notice, going about their business, continuing their conversations, only a few pointing and whispering. *What shall we do? Should we go over, offer to help?* No one ever did. Not until him. Until Stephen.

"Love, are you all right?" he'd said, pulling out a chair beside her.

Handsome. That was the first thing she noticed as she turned to look at him. He had dark eyes, and dark hair worn short and greased back. The smile on his face lit his eyes, highlighting the concern in them, for her, the crying girl, the broken one.

Immediately, she'd apologised. "I was just about to leave," she'd said, rising.

He'd risen too. "To go where?"

"Why…home of course."

"Where's home?"

She'd faltered, not because she was afraid to tell him, but because for a second she *didn't* want to go back. What kind of home was it without her parents?

"Wildacre," she'd said at last, having to say something. "A short drive away."

"You have a car?"

"Of course."

He'd mimicked her then. *Of course.* Causing her to frown.

"I really must go," she'd said, bending to pick up the goods she'd bought, sustenance for another month, barely.

"Here, let me help you," he'd said, also bending to grab the nearest bag.

"No. Thank you. I'm perfectly capable."

Their eyes had met, and it was as though she were caught in a vice.

"Please let me help you," he continued, an imploring note in his voice.

"Why?" she could only whisper back.

"Because you look as if you could do with some help. As if…you need it."

As he straightened, she noticed what he was wearing. Not smart clothes, those of a gentleman, a suit of some description – instead just trousers, a shirt, and a jacket. *Young clothes*, she supposed, according to the fashion of the day. An ordinary young man. But oh, those eyes! They captured her. *You need help,* he'd said, and suddenly she knew it to be true. She craved it.

He not only brought her shopping to the car, and loaded it, he accompanied her back to Wildacre.

"But how on earth will you get home?" she'd asked.

"I'll walk," he said with a shrug. "I like walking."

"It's miles!"

Again, he'd grinned. "I like walking a lot."

As she'd put the car into gear and driven away, with Stephen firmly in the passenger seat, she'd laughed. The sound of it startled her. She sounded…rusty, and immediately she fretted. Did he think so too?

She looked sideways at him. If he did, he gave no indication. He just continued to sit there, one arm resting almost nonchalantly against the door, looking happy, as if for all the world he belonged there, had taken his rightful place.

When she turned into the driveway at Wildacre, she could sense his surprise.

"Blimey," he said at last, on a whoosh of breath. "It's some place you've got here."

"Thank you."

"What did you say its name was?"

"Wildacre."

"Wildacre," he repeated, and the word sounded so soft on his lips. "Imagine that."

She'd parked the car in the driveway, switched off the engine, and quickly he exited, insisting he'd bring all the bags in. "You just open the door," he instructed.

At a loss what else to do, how to even begin to protest, she'd obeyed, and he'd followed shortly after, placing the bags down in the hallway.

His eyes were wide still as he looked around. "It's incredible. Although…"

"Although what?" she cajoled, curious at his delight.

"You could do with some paintings on the walls, you know, of yourself, your family, your…husband, maybe?"

Briefly, his eyes lowered to her hand. He'd done that before, in the café and in the car. Her *bare* hands. He already knew she wasn't married. Was he teasing her?

"I'm single," she clarified. "I have no husband, and no portraits of myself either."

"Okay, all right. What about your parents, though?" He swept an arm around him. "There should be plenty of portraits. You know, those ancestral ones. The lords and ladies of the manor, standing there, all hoity-toity. A cut above."

Such strange things he was saying, but with the gentlest of smiles on his face.

"I'm Stephen, by the way. I don't think we've formally introduced ourselves."

She took the hand he proffered, feeling how warm his skin was compared to hers.

"I'm an orphan," she said, unable to stop the words from

leaving her mouth, again worried what his reaction would be, whether he'd laugh at her or think her mad.

He simply continued to hold her hand, his grasp tightening a little.

"It's all right," he said, "it's okay. Want to know something? A little secret?"

"What?" she'd whispered back, enchanted by his kindness.

"I'm an orphan too."

# Chapter Sixteen

He never left. Stephen set foot in Wildacre, and he stayed. She couldn't believe it. Hadn't dared to hope. Every day believing she'd wake, and he'd be gone, that he was a dream she'd brought into being, taken from her as suddenly as her parents.

A miracle was how she thought of him. And with him she did indeed change, becoming someone she thought she would never be, not as wistful, or as dreamy, as otherworldly. She lived with him here, in this world, at Wildacre.

He loved her. Very quickly he said it. He loved the house too, *their* home, she called it, and it would make him smile.

Both orphans. Wildacre was a refuge he seemed to need as much as she did. She never asked about where he'd lived beforehand, or about the life he'd had, for what did it matter? The past was done, it was over with. A new chapter beginning.

The things he introduced her to! The touch of his hand gently caressing her, never rushing but taking his time, making her beg for something more.

"Stephen, please," she'd breathe, "I need you in all ways."

"Soon," he promised. "Believe me, my darling, we'll be joined in all ways soon."

Had her parents ever felt like this? So in love? They appeared to be, but it was an easy kind of love, the pair of them 'rubbing along' as her father would say, never a cross word between them, not that she'd ever been witness to. *Their* love, though, hers and Stephen's, was passionate. They *did* argue. About silly things. And always prompted by her. When he'd take the car, 'to go shopping' he'd say, 'to get food', she'd accuse him! God forgive her, but she'd do so with such a shrill voice!

"You're never coming back, are you? You're bored, that's it, yes. Bored already. Fine, I don't care. As long as I have Wildacre. This is my house, remember? Mine! I don't need you or anyone else. Go on! Go! You don't belong here. Just *me*."

She would hurl things at him. Whatever came to hand; things that had belonged to her parents and were therefore precious. Such objects would hurtle through the air, Stephen neatly sidestepping them, both watching as they fell and smashed.

"How many times do I need to tell you?" he'd shout back. "I'm going nowhere! And I do belong, here with you. I love it. I love you."

"And yet you won't make love to me!" she'd retort. "You sleep in that room at the end of the corridor, so chaste."

"Everything in good time, I've told you."

"When?" she'd scream.

"When the time is right," he'd say. "Look, darling, you need something to relax you. We both do. We barely know each other and yet…it's all so intense." There was a kind of hopelessness in his eyes when he'd said that, which further terrified her. "*Being here* is intense, so far from everyone."

"You said you loved it!"

"I do, but—"

143

"You're lonely. I'm not enough. It is that, isn't it?"

"It's not! It's just… Sometimes I think I hear voices, in the night, drifting on the atmosphere, and footsteps too."

Her heart had quickened to hear him say this. Was it them, her parents? She could no longer hear them – she had perhaps grown too attuned – but he, the newcomer, could? Were they…approving voices? Happy for her? What if they weren't? What if they were trying to scare him away, this imposter, and have her all to themselves? Yes, they'd encouraged her to mingle, but they'd never *pushed* her. "At least we never have to worry where she is," her mother had said to her father, another thing she'd overheard. "Some of the things young people get up to these days!" And her father would laugh. "Darling, young people have got up to things throughout the ages. It's naïve to think otherwise. But yes, yes, I agree. It's a headache we've avoided."

Despite her mood, Stephen dared to bridge the gap between them. Perhaps he could see how fearful she was, how feverishly her mind swung from one thought, one emotion, to another. An ordinary man. He seemed to have no money of his own, it was she that paid for everything. She didn't mind, though. She didn't! But sometimes she couldn't stop her traitorous mind from questioning even this. *Why have you sought me out? What is it you truly want from me?*

"Darling," he repeated, "I'm going to get us something so that we can both relax. Christmas is coming, our first, and I promise, it will be very special, our best yet. We just need to…relax. Be patient, for a little longer."

He kissed her and held her tighter. It was clear he knew perfectly well the effect he had on her, how weak at the knees she'd get. Then he left, and she tried to keep herself busy, trying not to notice how *crushingly* lonely it was without him.

There was a mirror hanging over the fireplace in the living room, and so she went there to look at herself, trying to see what Stephen could see. He'd told her many times how pretty she was, her skin as soft as velvet, blue eyes vibrant. She *was* pretty, she supposed, fair hair having grown out from the neat style she'd favoured, that she'd seen in her mother's magazines, now almost reaching her shoulders. There was an air about her, though, that concerned her. It was as though loneliness…*cleaved* to her, was something perfectly visible. She *wasn't* lonely, not any more. Stephen was here. He had been for several weeks, and was staying. And Christmas was coming. A special one, he'd said. The very best.

She'd bake whilst he was gone! Surprise him on his return with a cake. She'd fill this house with the most irresistible of aromas, her feet already moving towards the corridor, and reaching the hallway. There she stopped, but only briefly, en route to the kitchen, glancing up at the bare walls. *There should be portraits there, those fancy, ancestral ones.* He'd said something like that. Well there would be soon. She'd make sure of it. He'd have everything he desired at Wildacre.

When Stephen returned, he was delighted with the cake she thrust at him, but then told her to sit before he took a slice, that she too would be delighted with him. Not only had he bought food, he'd bought alcohol. Bottles and bottles of it.

"Why?" she'd asked.

"Because Christmas is coming!" he replied. "I've told you, we need to relax."

He'd then sat her down in the kitchen and pulled something from his jacket pocket, cradling it almost lovingly before showing her. It was a powder of some sort, in a cellophane bag. "This," he said, his dark eyes shining, "is what will truly help us do that, however. Darling, forget about unpacking. Let's take some now."

As sheltered as her upbringing had been, as removed from the real world, she knew what she was being offered – a drug of some sort – and she recoiled.

Ah, but Stephen could be persuasive! And he was right, she did need to unwind; right too about life being intense at Wildacre. If she wasn't careful, that intensity could drive him away. *Just the once,* she promised herself. *I'll try it just the once.*

He'd shown her how to take the drug, pushing bags of shopping further along the table as he'd done so. Having gone first, he whooped, and there she saw it – pure joy in his eyes! A joy that lit something in her too, that she wanted, something to push all doubt aside, every fear that lingered, that Wildacre could magnify.

That first time was magical. *Every* time was magical, subsequent days passing in a blur, a merry-go-round of laughter, eating, drinking, powder and pills. The supply of it all was endless. They would dance in the hallway, with music on the record player that her father had bought her mother, turned up loud. They would sleep, just sleep, in each other's arms, in the living room, a fire blazing before them as the weather raged outside, his voice whispering in her ear all the while, *You and me, darling, it's you and me, orphans in the storm who've found each other. We'll never be alone again. We belong here together, at Wildacre.* Words that were such a comfort. Then it happened: the proposal, on

Christmas Day, and the consummation of their love, falling asleep not in the living room but her bedroom, together, entwined. *Fused*.

The first time he'd touched her, *properly* touched her, she'd been…relaxed, as he'd called it, but still she remembered every second, committed to memory each stroke, each kiss. He was clearly an experienced man, despite being barely older than her, one more than willing to teach her everything he knew.

They married in a registry office, with two strangers as witnesses. They giggled their way through the short ceremony. The registrar was bemused by them.

As they left his office, Stephen tipped the strangers a handsome amount, laughing again at their surprised but thrilled reaction. Then it was back to Wildacre, where winter deepened, leaving them every bit as stranded as they wanted to be.

"We have everything we need, right here," he'd said one night, as they sat wrapped in blankets close to the window in the living room. There was another thick swathe of snow falling from above. A wonderland at their disposal.

"Promise me you won't get bored," she'd said, a tease and a plea in her voice.

"Bored?" he'd said. "Of this?"

"Of me, silly! Your wife."

He'd laughed then: a deep, throaty chuckle as he reached for a tumbler of whisky. "I won't get bored of you, wife. Promise not to get bored with me."

"I couldn't!" she breathed. "Life at Wildacre isn't for everyone. It is isolated here, I know it. But it has suited me, and it will suit us. You get…used to it. It's *real* life." She'd turned to him then, smelt the whisky on his breath, kissed his lips quickly, tasting it that way. "We've good times ahead, as long as we're together."

"We will be," he whispered, "and look at me. I have grown used to it, when I thought…" Rather than finish that sentence, he started another. "I love it – and you – more each day. I've told you, it's you and me forever. Just *us*."

Winter gave way to spring, which in turn bowed down to the majesty of summer. Days that were spent outdoors in the grounds of Wildacre. More music, more drinking, more relaxants. He'd leave the house for supplies. She barely would, but she no longer worried he wouldn't come back. She barely worried about anything.

It was during the summer that she'd had the painting of them commissioned, having left the house after all to venture back into Jedburgh, wanting to find details of someone suitable. It was Stephen who wanted the old-fashioned background, with him and her as Lord and Lady. A classical style, he called it.

The man who came to wield his brush whilst they'd stood together all dressed up, was called Thomas. He was around a similar age to them, and handsome too, in his own way. They tried hard not to giggle when having to pose, to focus when he told them to focus, to jut their chins dutifully this way and that. At first bemused by them, perhaps even a little frustrated, Thomas at last began to smile at their antics.

It was she who'd invited him to stay for dinner one evening, growing as comfortable in his company as she had in Stephen's, rushing off to concoct a dish whilst he cleaned brushes and tidied up. Although a confident artist, he was shy on the approach to the dinner table, again making them giggle. Stephen had sat him down, telling him that before eating, he needed something to help him relax.

Thomas stayed too, and it became the three of them when before it was two. He continued to paint them, to see out the long days with them, days she couldn't quite recall…that passed in such a warm haze. Until the argument, that was. What started it, she didn't know, but there it was: Stephen raging at Thomas, Thomas raging back.

"You've gone too far," Stephen accused.

"You encouraged me!" Thomas retaliated. "To get involved, to live here with you."

"Not to live, never to live!"

"That's not what you said. I remember."

"And you touched her. Intimately, you touched her."

"You encouraged me to do that too!"

Her head was swimming listening to them. Had Thomas touched her? Yes, of course he had, and not only the once. She'd enjoyed it, the attention of not one handsome lover but two. And…there was something else she must remember, that she had told herself to. The two men had touched each other, hadn't they? When she'd been sleeping, she'd heard them, their voices drifting towards her as voices did at Wildacre. She *knew* what they were doing. And yet she hadn't minded.

Life was different at Wildacre. It didn't follow the rules. What they were doing – Stephen and Thomas – wasn't wrong, not if it was in the name of love. There was so much love at Wildacre! It was a house built for it. So why now were they arguing, when the three of them were cut from the same cloth? United?

The argument continued to rage as she slept, wanting to return to a place where there wasn't this, a storm in the midst of summer.

Thomas left, but the painting stayed. She loved it! It was misty, ethereal, dreamlike, as life itself became once again. She missed Thomas, though; his initial shyness, his obvious awe of them. How that had tickled her!

She complained once to Stephen, as autumn set in, the cold air biting harder.

"Where is he? Why'd you do that, drive him away? I thought you liked him being here. I heard you, together. You know I did. I wasn't jealous, though. I was...*relaxed* about it. But you were jealous of me. And there was never any need. I'm yours, always and for ever. But he fit, you know? It was fun."

"No," Stephen had growled in her ear, whisky once again strong on his breath. "He didn't fit. No one else will. It's just us, at Wildacre. That's the way it works best. I understand that now. *Plainly* understand. It has to be just us."

# Chapter Seventeen

Sheltered. Naïve. She'd been all those things, but now she was to be something else besides. A mother. She'd only just realised her monthly cycles had stopped. A trip to the doctor when Stephen had been sleeping confirmed her suspicions.

*Just us*, was what Stephen had said. *That's the way it works best.* But now, there'd be an extension of them, and so he'd be pleased when she broke the news, surely? Even so, she was nervous about telling him over dinner that night. She thought she'd let him eat first and make sure he was relaxed, and then she blurted it out. His face had remained passive at first, with only his eyes betraying his shock, and then slowly…very slowly, acceptance edged its way in.

Such a relief! He was happy! So was she. They would talk about the baby, plan, getting a room ready for his or her arrival. Resolved to change their ways, not drink as much, smoke…or relax. That's what she had to remember later: they *both* tried.

The baby came. A girl – Amelia! Such a pretty name, one they'd chosen together. The most beautiful thing she'd ever seen, and he declared it was the same for him, quickly adding, 'Because she's so like you, darling. She's *exactly* like you.'

The house was filled with a noise otherwise alien to it. Screaming. Amelia suffered from colic. She wouldn't sleep, and had to be walked through the night, up and down, up and down. But she didn't mind, nor that Stephen always slept throughout it. She wanted to do this, look after her baby. She wanted another! To fill Wildacre with a family of her own, when before she'd had nothing, not even her parents.

A second baby arrived, this time a boy, born near Christmas, and so they called him Gabriel. A brother for Amelia. Life was different. Was…normal. Both she and Stephen embraced the change, the busyness of it. They would home-school the children, Stephen decided. No need for anything formal, to bring the outside in when they'd done without it for so long. She couldn't agree more.

Spring, summer, autumn, winter – the seasons changed, and changed swiftly. Life was passing so quickly, the children growing from babies to toddlers to small children. Contented children, children lavished with gifts from Stephen's trips into town, growing up within the sanctity of Wildacre. It was all they ever knew, and it was perfect. Laughter on everyone's lips. Their playground was the land that the house sat in. All four would charge out there, explore, marvel at the changing face of nature, then head back inside for warmth and shelter. *Just us*, she'd say to Stephen, echoing the very thing he'd say to her. *It should be just us at Wildacre. The four of us.*

That her life should be so transformed amazed her. She'd endured two years of loneliness, then loneliness was banished. She couldn't – wouldn't – wish for anything more.

So when did it change? When did the darkness, the bleakness, come creeping back in? Wildacre wasn't meant for darkness. It was her home, her world. *Theirs.*

*He* changed. Stephen. Became so restless. The trips he

made into town, for the sake of the children, he said, buying them more treats, became more frequent.

She'd challenged him again, about that, and also about being short-tempered with the children, which was something that was happening more often too.

"Stephen, is something wrong? I've not seen you like this before. You are happy, aren't you? Oh Stephen, we've so much to be happy about!"

How he had shouted at her! "For God's sake, stop asking me the same question all the time! Always, you nag me. I'm fine. Just fine. It's you that needs to…relax."

She was stunned. She never nagged him. She wanted to challenge him further, but the children had wanted to play. As she turned, she heard him mutter.

"That's it, leave me, why don't you? You put them first, always."

Things didn't improve. He lost weight, looked haggard. This, despite the meals she cooked. Good food, nourishing; the smell enticing to everyone but him.

She found him crying, in the living room, in front of the fire, winter having returned, wringing his hands together so hard, as he was prone to lately. She thanked goodness the children were in bed and wouldn't witness this.

Kneeling before him, she held onto his hands. "What is it? Tell me."

He hadn't answered, not straightaway. Not until she'd prompted him.

"I don't know," he admitted at last. "I…I miss the way it was. There's so much…responsibility now. So much…life."

Life? Responsibility? "Do you the mean the children?"

"You're always distracted."

"But Stephen—"

"Life is so intense here."

"It's our life. What we wanted. You and I both."

His head had come up. "I didn't ask you to get pregnant."

She'd gasped. "What are you saying? That you *regret* the children?"

Such conflict in his eyes! "Yes. No. I don't know… My head… I need something."

She reared back slightly. "You need to relax?"

His clutch on her tightened. "Yes! Just now and then, but I want us to relax together, like we used to. We've been such…model parents. You are… You're wonderful. But I need time alone with you. You remember, don't you? How we danced in the hallway? How we'd laugh? We can't let that go! What's between us is… special. I can't believe how special it is. *Nothing* must come between us."

"They're our children, Stephen!"

"I know, and we devote ourselves to them, day in, day out, but they're not babies any more. I miss you, darling. I want what we had. I *liked* it that way."

It had been so long since she'd relaxed, since she'd drunk anything, but Stephen was right. They needed a little time just for them. She'd resolved once to do anything it took to please him, and so she must fulfil that promise.

How different it was this time. As enjoyable as before. *Too* enjoyable. She never realised how stressed she was, not until the stress dissolved. She loved the children, with all her heart, playing with them, exploring, crafting, but oh, Stephen was a genius! Because she loved this too, the way it used to be. She began to need it, as much as she'd ever needed anything in her life, sleeping so well afterwards, for far too long, perhaps. Hours and hours passing, the children left to their own devices, running wild. But then, wildness was what the house was all about.

Drugs and a family – the two could mix, couldn't they? Perhaps not in the real world, but at Wildacre, anything was possible. They *did* mix. They got along just fine. The atmosphere was happy again. More importantly, Stephen was happy.

Stuff was disappearing, she was certain of it. Stuff which hadn't been broken in arguments or their careering clumsiness, as the pair of them crashed into sideboards and tables when dancing. She had no idea why things were going missing, until she caught him leaving the house with yet more of Wildacre's possessions in his hands.

"We need the money," he'd explained.

"But we have money," she protested. "Stephen, we're not poor!"

How sheepish he'd looked, but he was also determined. "Love, we don't need this stuff. It's theirs, your parents. It's…old-fashioned. No. Better to have the money. Go on now, go back inside. It's cold out here. You'll catch your death."

And she'd obeyed, confused still but wondering if he was right. She'd check her accounts soon, one day, when she had time. When the children weren't calling out for her; hungry, always hungry. When she could focus.

It was one day in late autumn she had the idea! She'd go back to Jedburgh, this time with the children. She'd tell Stephen she was shopping for Christmas, preparing well in advance, buying a present, she said, that she knew he'd like. Groggy. All his responses were lately. Her own were often the same. But for the town visits, she'd spruce herself up,

155

apply make-up, excited about what she had planned. There was money enough in the pot for this, she was sure of it.

The unveiling was when darkness tightened its grip. On Christmas Eve. Two portraits – one of Amelia, one of Gabriel – painted to match the style of their portrait. There was a dreamy quality about them, with the children's innocence perfectly captured: a slight smile on Gabriel's face, although Amelia was more pensive.

Thank goodness the children were in bed when she'd shown him. He'd struck her, hard, across her mouth. The first time he'd ever lifted his hand to her.

"Stephen!" she'd screamed, both shocked and bewildered.

"You've been seeing him, Thomas!"

She shook her head, scrabbled away from him when he advanced further. "It's a different artist, I just…I asked him to paint in the same way as Thomas, so they'd match our painting. And look, Stephen, they do! Exquisite, aren't they?"

"No!" he'd yelled at her, "they will never hang there, never! It should be just us. How many times must I tell you? I can't believe you've wasted our money like this."

Something in her had hardened. *Our* money?

"Grow up, Stephen! There is no *just us*, not anymore. The portraits of Amelia and Gabriel will hang beside ours. They will! Life has changed. We're a family. We must act like one again. We have to. Stephen, I can barely think any more, or function. No, I've decided. There should be no more drugs, no more…relaxing. We have to take responsibility for what we've done, for the lives we've created, as well as our own lives. Put the money in the coffers to good use, *their* inheritance. Please, darling, we can't go on like this, don't you see? The house is a wreck, you're…emptying it. Day by day by day. It looks abandoned when it isn't. We will live here, the four of us, in our world, yes, a world we've created, but not like this, not any more. We will live as my parents did, respectably."

He had listened to every word, and she was pleased about that, that he seemed to consider what she said, that it was sinking in. But what he did next caused fear to bloom as cold as any winter at Wildacre. The way his eyes didn't rest on her, but instead flickered upwards to the ceiling, towards where the children's room was.

"Just us," he repeated, his expression like thunder.

# Chapter Eighteen

## *24<sup>th</sup> December – Christmas Eve*

During the earlier part of the story, Isla had drifted, entranced by the tale unfolding, feeling every emotion Jessica must have felt. Her sense of loss after the sudden death of her parents, the loneliness that had ensued, the love that had then developed between her and Stephen, something out of the blue that had struck hard, the…debauchery. That's when she'd sat up again, began to take more notice, hanging on every word. There *had* been love between Jessica and Stephen. She didn't doubt that, and Jessica hadn't, but something had happened to that love. In the confines of Wildacre, a world removed, it had grown darker. A need for something more had made itself known, beyond the excitement of new love, of children. A desire for other thrills, to recapture the hedonism that responsibility had destroyed.

*Just us* was what Stephen kept saying, kept insisting on – this man who had come to Wildacre and never left. A man with…appetites. With urges he could control but only for so long, that he'd also introduced Jessica to – she who was as much an innocent as Amelia and Gabriel were, all of them caught in the storm. Orphans. Was Stephen really an orphan, as he claimed? Or was he a loner, a chancer?

Someone who saw an opportunity and seized it? A possessive man, although Jessica was possessive as well. What was the purpose of selling off all that he could? And when he'd finally murmured *just us,* his eyes on the ceiling, what – or whom – did he mean by it?

"Jessica," she said, when the woman grew quiet, staring at the door now when before she'd been gazing only into the past, "what happened to the children? To Stephen? How did they die?"

It had taken Jessica so long to tell the story that daylight was fading. Long shadows were being cast in the room, but shadows that remained static…for now.

"Jessica, tell me. And…" she too glanced at the door, "…tell me quickly."

Tears were trickling down Jessica's face. "I'm sorry. So sorry."

Rising from Amelia's bed, Isla stepped closer. "I know. I know you are, but, Jessica, it's time. Confess."

"Confess?" she said, her eyes on Isla now. Isla swallowed hard on seeing how blurred they were. No longer focused.

"Jessica, come on, stay with me. Don't slip. Remember what we were talking about, okay? About Stephen, and your children too, Amelia and Gabriel. You have to stay with me, Jessica, because…because…" her gaze strayed back to the door, and the handle that rattled. She caught Jessica by the shoulders. "They were going to leave you, weren't they? Stephen was selling stuff off to feather his own nest. That's the saying, isn't it? Wanting a place of his own that wasn't Wildacre, another refuge. He did that because…because…it would never be the same between you, not now that the children were here. Having children changes everything. I've heard my parents say it often enough, that whole dynamic.

He'd accumulated his own stash of money, stripped the place bare, right in front of your eyes, but he wouldn't leave alone. He'd take the children with him. Why, I don't know. Because he loved them, truly, deep down, when he was sober at least, when he could think straight, or because he wanted to hurt you, or because he was a man so mixed up, so lost, he didn't know what he was doing. Not any more. It could even have been that the children were his return ticket should it all go wrong on the outside, should he find he'd grown too used to Wildacre, and couldn't cope. Without them, you might refuse him, but you'd never refuse them. You *wanted* to do your best by them. As you said, you tried, but addiction, and not just to the drugs, got in the way, time and time again. Oh, Jessica, he was going to leave you. And you remembered all too well the loneliness of Wildacre after your parents died. And you couldn't stand it. Wouldn't."

Not just the handle, the entire door rattled.

"Wait!" Isla yelled, not at Jessica but to whomever was listening. "You can just bloody well wait, okay? If it is Stephen, you're as much to blame for this. Maybe…maybe you don't deserve to leave. Not then and not now. Or maybe it's truer to say you never deserved to be here in the first place." Turning back to Jessica, she shook her, but gently. "Don't get stuck here, okay? Not you. And don't keep the children here either. It's been too long, and it's not fair. It's no way for them to exist. As for Stephen, you might have destroyed his face in that portrait, destroyed *him*, but anger can't destroy love, or the memory of it at least. He's here, and he's as angry as you, as bewildered. Jessica, you're dying, you know that, don't you? You haven't got long left. Maybe…hours. It's Christmas Eve. They all died on Christmas Eve, didn't they? Because that's when he tried to leave. Such a cruel time of year to do something like that, the very worst. Jessica, how did you try to stop them?"

If Jessica was going to answer, she never got a chance. Once again, the door gave way under the pressure of what was behind it. Blackened energy entered the room. A storm; Jessica caught up in it, and Isla too, the pair clinging to each other, their screams joining the roars but easily swallowed.

The children's toys, their dolls, their teddies, their trains, the tree that had survived everything – Isla, just too afraid to open her eyes, had no idea if they were caught up in the maelstrom. But she was moving, her feet carrying her forwards, *they* were, she and Jessica, towards the door, her head hanging low, but it didn't matter. She knew the way, as if she'd trodden this route a thousand times before.

They reached the landing. Jessica was muttering and wailing. *Oh God, Oh God, Oh God.* The words on everyone's lips in times of desperation. And *I'm sorry. So sorry.*

Where should they go? What should they do? The storm that was behind them, in the house rather than outside it, continued to unburden itself, fury seeking its final release, intent only on ruin. *Their* ruin, alongside his.

*Where the hell do we go?*

If she thought she'd have to drag Jessica down the hallway, to the stairs, she was wrong. The woman fought free of Isla's grip, began moving at a pace that Isla would have previously considered impossible.

"Where are you going?" she yelled, horrified to see her not heading downstairs, but further down the corridor, past her own bedroom, to the one at the far end. His bedroom: Stephen's, earmarked by him when he'd first arrived, making Jessica wait for his touch, to desire him beyond all reason, for ever more.

161

And it worked. She had.

It was the room that housed the portrait. The one of just the two of them.

"Wait!" She started yelling at Jessica. "He'll come there. Come after us. We have to go downstairs and get out of here!" Away from Wildacre. But that would mean away from the children too. The true innocents. "Oh, Jessica!"

She picked up speed and followed her, hearing something other than Stephen as she ran: a scampering. Smaller feet that kept pace with hers, then overtook.

On entering the room, she saw them, the children, as wispy and as dreamlike as their portraits, huddled in the corner, their eyes impossibly wide.

Useless to beg Jessica to leave. She wouldn't. Not even with her dying breath.

There she was, the old woman, on the floor, her arms wrapped around the desecrated painting that stood propped against the chest of drawers, crying and muttering. Only the face of her younger self was smiling, shining with love.

"I'm sorry, sorry, sorry," she said. "But you were going to leave me. All of you."

Stephen was coming towards Isla as she stood in the doorway, she knew it. That same something that had been in the children's room, having depleted itself, and so *crawling* up the hallway, gathering energy, gathering *intent*.

"What did you do, Jessica?" Isla said, surprised that her voice sounded so firm when she was shaking so hard, when her heart and soul had shrivelled inside her. "How did you kill them? How did you kill yourself? Because in effect, that's what you did. Denied yourself the right to live too. Jessica, stop your crying and tell me!"

Although Jessica still clung to the painting, her shoulders

eased. It took precious moments which Isla feared they didn't have, but eventually she began talking.

"So quickly. It all happened so quickly."

"What did, Jessica? What?"

"I… I…"

"Remember, Jessica. Remember everything. They're here, you know that as well as I do, you've as good as admitted it. Stephen, Amelia, and Gabriel. Listening. Because…I think they want to know too. They're unsure of what happened because it was so…sudden. Was that it? Everything went dark so quickly."

Murmurings, murmurings, murmurings, but then more intelligible words followed.

"It *was* Thomas I commissioned to paint the children's portraits. I lied to Stephen about that. It was nice to see him, but it was innocent! Do you hear me? Innocent! He'd matured, he was married, and was happy in his marriage. Or so he told me. But I saw it, on a shelf in the studio he had now: a vase, so like the one my parents used to own. I was certain of it, at least at the time I was. Now…I'm not so sure. Whenever I went there, it seemed to glare at me, to tell a story of its own. Stephen had accused me of sleeping with Thomas, being unfaithful, when…when… His anger at the unveiling confirmed my suspicions: *he* was the one who'd betrayed *me*."

Jessica had been eyeing Isla when speaking, but now she looked beyond her. The space was not empty, and she hissed at what she saw.

"Even if I was wrong about the vase, and about Thomas, I was never enough for you. Always, you wanted something more. When I realised what you were going to do, I came out with it, threw your accusation right back at you. How stunned you were! Raising your hand to hit me again, although I avoided the blow that time. Deluded, that's what you said I was. And that I always had been. 'Too much,' you kept saying, 'this is all too much. We're…destroying each other.' If we hadn't had children, it might have been different, you continued, but even then, you suspected the rot would have set in, that nothing stays the same, absolutely nothing. I railed against you as you continued to climb the stairs, flew at you to strike back, but so easily you caught my hand. Above us I could hear the children running to their room, like they'd run a hundred times before lately. You'd put a lock on their door, and when I enquired about it, you said it was to protect the children. From whom, Stephen, whom? There was no one here but us!"

Still Jessica was clutching at the portrait, still staring beyond Isla.

"I remember…I remember you said we'd been out of control for too long, and that I was right, we had to take responsibility. Things had changed and we should both just accept it, live differently, the old ways no longer fit for purpose. But it was you that introduced me to the drugs! And when we stopped, because of the children, it was you who wanted to restart. Because you were bored! Because I wasn't enough. Because it was all too intense," she mimicked. "And so you'd take the children, *my children*, and leave me. 'So you can pull yourself together,' you said. It was you who tore me further apart! A stranger who burst into my life and took over."

"Jessica…" Isla began… Such coldness at the back of her heel. Stephen had made contact, a hand that would soon creep more fully around her ankle, and drag her down, down, down with him, into the cold dark ground where he was, then return for Jessica. *Just us*, but she'd be part of it, Isla, joining them. Her legs gave way at such a terrible prospect, aiding and abetting Stephen in his aim, forcing her to cling to the doorframe to remain upright.

Stephen was guilty of many things, but he was *not* a murderer. She had to remember that. She forced herself to speak again. "How did you kill them, Jessica?"

"He ran up the stairs," Jessica answered readily enough. "Went first to his room to grab a bag. One that was already packed! I tried to stop him, kept screaming at him, and he was roaring back at me. Then he raced back down the corridor, all the way to their room, the children's, kicked the door open and dragged Amelia and Gabriel from their beds. The screaming! Oh, the screaming. Can you hear it? Even now? All our screams. Mine, the children, and his, when once there'd been such laughter. How had it all gone so wrong? How can love turn to hate? I couldn't stop him. I tried, but I was cast aside. I begged him, threatened him. All of it fell on deaf ears. He was crying. I saw that, as outside he bundled the children into his car, and locked the doors. 'Why?' I kept asking. 'Why? Why? Why?' He turned then, finally allowing me an answer. 'It isn't me that's done this to you, it isn't the drugs, it's this house, it's Wildacre.' He said…he said that when he saw it, he couldn't believe his luck, or that I allowed him to stay, never asking him either who he was, or where he'd come from. I'd just…accepted him. He was alone in life, that much was true, just as I was, but here was an opportunity to live, really live, to never want for anything again. I'd fallen in love with him straightaway; for him it took time. But his feelings developed. Thomas made him realise that he didn't want to share me with another. He was content with it being just us. And then came the children. Children he didn't want, hadn't bargained for. But he loved them too. I know he did. You can't fake love!

"Stephen, though, wasn't used to life at Wildacre like I was, like the children were, the three of us having known very little else. He felt more and more of an outcast, like *he* wasn't enough. And then when I kept disappearing with the children… Oh, how the mind takes over at Wildacre! He never wanted responsibility, he said, and now it was heaped on him. 'Leave the children, then,' I screamed, 'what do you want them for?' But he wouldn't, because he said I was mad, and that if he stayed he'd succumb to madness too, and so would the children. 'This is a mad world we've forged, that I was mad to take on.' How tearful he was! How the children howled. 'Mummy! Mummy!' they screamed. 'What's happening?' I couldn't answer, and this time neither could Stephen, as confused as I was, perhaps, wondering how we'd let this happen, what we'd done to our minds, how messed up we were. I've said no rules applied at Wildacre, and it's true. There were never any limits.

"He left with the children. On Christmas Eve, at nearly midnight. A time when they should be caught up in the sweetest of dreams, excited for the morning to come, for more indulgence – all of us adored indulgence, *all* of us – not just me."

More sobs wracked Jessica, her thin frame slumping over, so frail, so old, and yet so much had lived inside her, every kind of emotion.

"They left," she said, finally lifting her head, "and…and…I turned back, looked at the house, and the darkness that wrapped itself around it, the loneliness. I could hardly bring myself to go back in there, not alone, not again, but it was only briefly. I had my own car, albeit until recently rarely used. I grabbed my keys, tried not to listen to the screams still caught in the atmosphere, that rattled around in my head, Amelia and Gabriel yelling for me, wanting their mother, even if their mother was what he'd said she was. Mad. Delusional. A drunk and an addict. I was addicted to him! Stephen. And he…he was addicted to me. I wasn't deluded about that. But the truth was something that became distorted at Wildacre, for both of us. We couldn't tell what was real any more, and what wasn't. I ran to the car, turned the engine over, put my foot down, and I screeched out of Wildacre, down that gravel driveway, and on to the road, determined to do one thing: bring them all back. We'd make it work. Find a way, *new* ways. Try and try again. Live and die at Wildacre. Just us."

"Oh, Jessica," Isla was the one who murmured now.

Jessica's voice was equally soft as she recalled further.

"I was crying so hard. The kind of tears that blind you. It was raining. There was fog, growing thicker, almost as white as snow. My whole world had been reduced further, to the size of the windscreen. The wipers blurred everything, just as my mind was blurred." As she'd done so often, she clutched at the neck of her nightdress. "I didn't…I don't know why he stopped the car, further down the lane." Lifting her head, she again looked beyond Isla. "I've thought about it since, when I can bear to. When the fog that persists even now clears a little. You stopped because…you'd changed your mind? Couldn't bear to leave, after all?"

A howl of anguish in Isla's ear caused her to take a deep breath. Jessica flinched as if she'd heard it too.

"Yes, yes," she continued. "You'd changed your mind. As I've said, every bit the addict too. You wanted to break away, felt you couldn't cope sometimes, but you were as hopelessly in love as I was. Hopelessly…I don't use that word lightly. You'd changed your mind, proved a point, reminded me how much I wanted you, because you were addicted to that too, the power, and you were coming back. Oh God, God, God…" Despair reached an even blacker point. "I'm sorry. So sorry. I just…didn't see that they'd stopped, not until it was too late, until I was upon them, the children, in the back seat, their faces turned towards me, waving, waving, *desperately* waving. I was going so fast! I ploughed into his car, into them, killed them. All of them. And you're right, dear, whoever you are: in that instant I killed myself, even though I escaped the wreckage and walked away from it with barely a scratch. A murderer, like you said I was, although others called it an accident. A terrible, terrible accident. The children were brought back here, as you know, and buried. Stephen also. His grave is next to theirs, unmarked. I hated myself, but oh I hated him too, for what he'd made me do, but still…I couldn't let go. Despite everything, this is where we belong. I know it. He knows it. We all do. Oh, the children! The children!"

"Jessica!" Isla shouted as the woman tried to stand, but instead collapsed further on to the ground. Whatever had been at her heel showed mercy. The hand retracted, enabling her to rush forwards, to tend to the living, her mind trying to process everything she'd been told, and what to do for the best.

Isla held Jessica, gently rubbing at her arms and patting her cheek. But all efforts to revive her were too late. The woman was growing cold, so cold.

"It was an accident," Isla told her, "not murder. You didn't mean it to happen."

"I killed them is all I know," Jessica whispered back, "but don't fret, dear, don't worry. Maybe, via my slow suicide, I've atoned. And maybe… I can atone further. Help me to sit up, please, one last time. Stephen? Stephen, where are you?"

Vehemently, Isla shook her head. "Jessica, no! Don't do that. Don't call him! He's dangerous, he wants revenge."

"He's *had* revenge, don't you think? And I have too. Do as I ask…help me sit up."

A dying wish that Isla granted, tentatively manoeuvring her to face the doorway.

"Stephen," Jessica said, before Isla could beg him to show more mercy, to leave them alone, not try to hurt them further. "Stephen, just…remember the good times we shared. The magic. Don't dwell on all that went wrong. Oh, I know I've dwelt on it, but we shouldn't, not any more. Good times…between you and I, and all four of us. The laughter…happened. Children, children, there, there, my darlings, come closer. I can see you so well now! Don't huddle in the corner like that…so small…so pitiful. Giggle, like you used to. I know you've not forgotten. You made the rafters shake! You stayed, not because I made you, but because this was our world. We can leave it now, though, if you wish. Yes, yes, we can. At Christmas. Our best yet."

They were there, the children. Isla had seen them, huddled in the corner. And Stephen had been there too, in the doorway, at her heel. She looked for them again, her head whipping from side to side. Where were they now?

"Jessica…?"

The old woman in her arms laughed, a bright, merry sound.

"That's it, darlings, closer still. I'm sorry I made you wait for so long, just…so confused. No longer. We deserve peace. We deserve…release." Her hands having reached out, it was as if though they were being clasped. "Thank you for never giving up, even though there were times when I did exactly that, when I rid the house of everything that was left in it," she whispered. "*Almost* everything. As bewildered, as angry and as sad as you all were, you didn't leave me. Not again." Teary eyes, full of wonder, focused back on Isla. What she said next was even more shocking.

"Burn it."

Isla gasped. "Burn what?"

"Wildacre."

"The house? Are you…? No! You can't be serious."

"Am I mad? No, dear, I think I'm finally sane. They're growing impatient, the children, and Stephen too, not willing to wait any longer, so listen… Listen! Raze this place to the ground. I…" A deep rattle in her throat caused her to splutter, but quickly she recovered, a determined woman who wouldn't be denied. "There was so much good here, but there was darkness too, and anguish. There were mistakes. And, in the end, just too much loneliness. No one should live here. Not after us."

"Jessica," Isla managed, overwhelmed again by all that was happening.

"Burn it!" Jessica repeated, rallying slightly in Isla's arms. "As Stephen said, nothing lasts for ever, not the good times, or the bad, not the sunshine, or the storms. Not even Wildacre. It's all so…fleeting really, except love. Love is the one thing that can endure. Burn Wildacre. Stop it from harming others."

Jessica's eyes widened, and even in such a gloom-ridden room Isla could tell they were brimming with happiness, no guilt there, no shame.

"Whoever you are, burn it," she repeated. "You're not a murderer either, no, no. You're an angel. You stayed too. But don't let anything hold you back now…fly."

A last inhalation, and then silence fell again at Wildacre. After a while Isla lifted her head towards the window, noticing snow softly falling rather than incessant rain.

# Chapter Nineteen

## 25<sup>th</sup> December – Christmas Day

Downstairs, in the living room, with midnight long gone, and the fire in the grate blazing, what logs there were piled high, Isla sat and considered. 'Burn it,' Jessica had said, this once beautiful house, this house of memories. The final purge.

She was gone, Jessica Lockhart, and she'd taken Stephen, Amelia and Gabriel with her. Had she grounded them with her guilt, her anguish, her sorrow and desire, or had they indeed stayed of their own free will, because they were family and that's what families did, looked out for each other no matter what, blood thicker than water? Who knew? She had the answers to some of it, but not all. She hadn't even believed in ghosts before Wildacre. But ghosts of the past? That was a different matter. They *did* hang around, and could be resurrected on a whim. Hauntings, it seemed, took many forms, Isla finally admitting that she was something haunted too. As lonely as Jessica had ever been. And it frightened her...how loneliness could turn to desperation, and desperation to madness.

Should she burn this house, with Jessica's body in it? She could get into serious trouble for doing that, unless...unless they deemed it an accident. Even so, no. She wouldn't do it.

Couldn't. *They don't pay me enough for this shit.* A wry thought, one she'd had many times since being there, but which failed to cause even an ounce of amusement. She would just go, she decided. Turn her back on this place once and for all: walk out of the wilderness and towards civilisation. It didn't matter how long it took her to reach help, not any more, or how hard the snow was falling outside, and how cold she'd get. She'd call the police as soon as she could and tell them about Jessica, that her charge had died, of natural causes, nothing more.

The second person in her care to do so.

Would they believe her?

Would she be blamed as much as she blamed herself?

She leant back against the sofa. God, she was tired! And so, so confused.

Jessica's final wish, it really was too much to ask for.

"I'm sorry, Jessica," she whispered, her eyes forcing themselves shut, the heat in the room like a tranquilliser. What did it matter if she slept? Why fight it?

Her mind was feverish again, and little wonder. *It's this house making you sick.* Could a house really do that? Something built of bricks and mortar, not something sentient. Memories *were* sentient, though. They had a life of their own, and what were houses but vessels for memories? A testament to the lives people had lived within them: the glorious times, and the less than glorious.

*Burn it down.*

*Fly.*

So hard to do either.

Dreams came, but remained muddled. She was in corridors, inside herself, a body like a house too, full of paths you didn't want to roam down, fearful of what might jump out at you. She dreamt of the clients she tended – *people*, her brain instantly screamed at her, don't call them clients! – who were also shells, most of them; sitting in the same seat, day after day, barely communicating, barely eating, unable to see to their own personal care. And yet they'd lived lives, all of them, *experienced* life, so many tales, so many anecdotes harboured, so many lessons they could impart if anyone should ever take the time to sit and listen. Had any of them loved, like Jessica had loved, so completely? Not just Stephen, or Amelia or Gabriel, but this house too – her first mad love. *I can't burn it, Jessica. I won't.*

*Angel. She called me an angel.* That thought at least took hold, the miracle of it. Christmas was a time for miracles, wasn't it? *I'm no angel, though.*

Sleep coaxed her further, time something that was both immaterial and passing, the snow outside getting deeper too, perhaps. Restorative sleep. Sleep which she'd wake feeling refreshed from, better. But braver too?

No answer to that either.

*I can't burn anything except bridges. No way back when you've done that.*

Wonderful sleep, the sleep of the dead. If that were so, then she was in good company. Was she smiling in her sleep, laughing at the joke she'd made, no matter it was in bad taste considering the circumstances? Perhaps. For she could hear laughter echoing around her, just as she used to. And the scampering of feet.

The scenes that played in her head! So many faces all blending into one another, strangers that she'd tended to, that gazed right through her; family members that she reached for, but who turned away. Or was it she who had turned from them?

No more faces, but a mist, obscuring everything, and comfort in that, rather than always striving for clarity, examining the facts over and over and yet reaching no conclusion. A mist that was getting…thicker. That felt like it was suffocating her. Was that it? Her chest was straining and her throat was catching, even in sleep.

No matter. She'd continue sleeping. Couldn't *resist* sleeping. Deeper and deeper.

No thoughts, no mist, just darkness, and Isla suspended in it.

Christmas Day – a time for peace, granted at last.

Why then was someone trying to snatch it from her? A sensation of something, a prodding, refusing to let her remain in such easy suspension, growing more urgent. Such *cold* fingers that jabbed, as cold as Stephen's hand had been around her heel, as the children's hands had been too. Whisperings. She also heard them.

*Wake up! Wake up!* The voice of a man, then another overriding it: a female, one with a hint of triumph in it. *It's burning.*

What was? The house? *No,* she wanted to tell whoever it was. *It isn't. I refused.*

The iciness from the prodding hands seemed to find its way inside, delivering a freeze shock to all her organs and kick-starting her heart.

She woke in another fit of coughing, with one hand clutching at her throat and the other trying to wipe spittle from her mouth. Her throat was on fire! Breath was fighting for expulsion, then fighting to be drawn in again. Inhaling what…smoke?

*What the hell?*

From having slumped, she pushed herself upright: a

simple gesture, but one which took so much effort. Her lungs protesting; more violent hacking. Her eyes were streaming too, almost – but not quite – blinding her.

Flames had escaped the grate! They were leaping all around her, spreading rapidly, growing taller, wilder, and just so gleeful. It was a sight both horrifying and beautiful. Mesmerising, like the house itself, like them, the family that had lived there.

*How, though? How?*

She'd built the logs up high, but securely enough. Had one rolled out, despite her efforts? Or had it been tugged at, to lie on the rug there, *encouraged* to take hold?

Remembering the cold hands, the voices that had whispered, Isla looked around, but could see nothing, only flames quickly multiplying. So effortlessly they took hold, devouring furniture, dancing up curtains, skittering along the floor.

Isla rose at last. "Jessica? Was this you?" Such a determined woman, but a woman who had saved her, or a family who had. They didn't want her to burn alongside Wildacre, or them. She had to escape, but how? The flames were surrounding her.

She had to run, that was how. Through the flames. Charge out of the door.

Or…she could stay. Sink back onto the sofa, close her eyes and sleep. It'd be a painless death if the smoke got to her before the flames did. As her legs buckled, more whispers started up, murmurings in her ear, and each one clearer than the last.

*Think, girl, think! Of all the things you haven't experienced, the life that could be lived. There'll be pain, there'll be guilt, more shame even, but there could also be such glory. Live for us when we couldn't, when we forgot how to. It's Christmas. Fly.*

Her heart jolted. It was Jessica again, in her head. Perhaps she'd *always* be there, in some form, but with advice like that, *sane advice*, that was no bad thing.

*Fly! Fly! Fly! It should be just us here.*

She would fly, through the flames, to safety. Choose life with all its vagaries, if life should be granted.

Head down, Isla charged, a roar escaping her, one whose intensity echoed through the house it.

Once through the doorway, she patted wildly at herself, convinced flames had engulfed her limbs and set her hair alight; relieved when it was only imagination. She'd escaped the worst of it, surely? Her eyes told her not, taking in the impossible.

There were flames everywhere! The house was engulfed.

*Fly!*

Through more flames?

She did it. She charged a second time, down the corridor, into the hallway, only briefly glancing at the wall there. The fire was licking greedily at the portraits. The one that was hanging in between the children showed the face of the man, Stephen, not ruined at all, but smiling back at Jessica, with a love that did indeed match hers. This woman, his prey, who'd then become so much more.

A crash from deep within the house startled her, telling her that yet again, time was running out. She continued to run, not quite knowing if all she'd seen in the house – the children, the shrine, the portrait, even Jessica herself – was all down to imagination or a dream, and that she'd wake soon, *properly* wake, to find herself still in her car, in a ditch, with her head badly bruised.

Fly. That's what angels did, and so she would. Although

flames skittered around the entrance too, the door was open. More strangeness, as she would never have left it like that. *What a strange place you are, Wildacre. What a…wild place.*

She ran, and it was as though a thousand hands were propelling her this time, along floorboards that would soon splinter and turn to ashes, towards freedom.

She screamed as she passed through the door, feeling the pressure at her back immediately release as she emerged the other side, showered with ashes and soot that again blinded her. She could only see properly when she was metres from the house, and had fallen onto the snow-covered ground, coughing and crying and wiping at her eyes, as much a blackened thing as Stephen had ever been. Stephen who'd changed his mind. Who would have stayed. Who did.

"You all fly!" she screamed when she could. "Can you hear me still? Fucking fly."

The flames danced higher at her words.

Moments passed that could have been minutes or hours. Isla was able to do nothing but watch Wildacre burn, adding to the burial site. She was entranced again, drifting, not even flinching when it was the building this time that roared. There were voices too, behind her, that took time to register.

"Miss! Miss! Oh my God, are you all right? Miss! It's okay! We're here. Shit, look at this! This…this is…terrible."

Confused, aching, tired, Isla at last turned around, to see not one person running towards her, but two. Other life entering Wildacre.

She shook her head as they continued to shout out, unable to trust her eyes, like Wildacre's predecessors, not knowing what was real and what wasn't, deciding, as the woman hunkered next to her, that reality didn't matter.

"She…" Isla said, as the woman continued to fuss over

her, "…she's in there."

The woman looked even more horrified. "Oh my God, what? Did you just say someone's in there?"

"She's…dead. Natural causes. I was her…carer."

"Shit!" The woman started yelling at the man with her. "Terry! Terry! Did you hear that? There's someone in the house!"

"What, really?" He'd been on the phone, but now he joined them. "There can't be. I've passed this house loads of times. Rumour is it's empty, that it's a probate matter or something, ongoing. But…whatever the case is, don't worry, okay? Just keep calm. We all have to keep calm. I've called 999. Help is on the way."

The woman half-lifted Isla to her feet, not letting her go, not for one minute.

"Other than you two," Terry asked, "there was no one else in there?"

"No. No one."

"You're okay?"

"I'm fine. There was a fire in the grate, in the living room. I fell asleep in front of it. I never thought…" Sobs burst from her, the woman quickly hugging her.

"Don't worry, don't worry," she kept murmuring. "It's all right. It's all right. It was an accident, that's what it sounds like, these things happen. Come on, come and sit in our car while we wait." Isla felt the shivers coursing through the woman's body. "God, it's so cold out here!" She then looked around her, at the burning hulk, and the countryside that surrounded it, pure white and blood orange. "So bloody desolate."

In the car, the woman continued to soothe Isla.

"We'll have you home soon, just as soon as the police and

the fire brigade arrive. Oh, listen, I can hear them, can you? They're almost here. It's so lucky we found you, that we came by. We'd been on a night out, then decided on a whim to visit Terry's grand-aunt. We thought we'd surprise her in the morning, you know, for Christmas. She's as crabby as they come, Terry's the first to admit it; she has a knack of rubbing people up the wrong way, but you know what, we love her to bits anyway. It amuses us how feisty she is, so old and still such a warrior. She's on her own. Wasn't supposed to be, but, long story short, there'd been some problems. So, yeah, we decided to head over. No one should be alone on Christmas Day, should they?"

Such a lot of words, tumbling from the woman's mouth, only some filtering into Isla's brain as the sound of the sirens grew louder. A flurry of vehicles would soon be turning off that narrow lane, winding their way past those ivy-ridden pillars, and up the gravel driveway, to a house that Terry at least thought was abandoned.

"My name's Belinda," the woman continued. "What's yours?"

"Isla," she answered, rubbing at her eyes.

"What's the name of the woman who lived there? Just so we can tell the police."

"Jessica Lockhart."

Terry, who'd also climbed into the front seat of the car, turned to look at her.

"Sorry, what did you say?" he said.

Isla cleared her throat, sniffed hard. "I said her name was Jessica Lockhart."

"Impossible," Terry insisted, his eyes not on Isla but Belinda, who was frowning every bit as hard as he was.

Isla glanced at the pair of them, her head pounding now,

due to the smoke, and the screech of the sirens only metres away. "Why?"

"Because that's Terry's aunt's name," Belinda told her, "the one I was just telling you about, that we're going to visit, so we can surprise her tomorrow morning. *She's* Jessica Lockhart, so…you know…whoever you've been caring for, it isn't her."

# Chapter Twenty

## *30<sup>th</sup> January*

Lydia Whittle, née Manklow, had been her name.

According to investigations carried out so far, Wildacre had been her family home. A tragic accident had indeed happened close to there in 1960, with Amelia Whittle, Gabriel Whittle and Stephen Whittle pronounced dead at the scene of a car crash. A crash that Lydia Whittle was also involved in, having ploughed into the back of her family's car in another vehicle, not registering, due to the bad weather, that the car was stationary. It had been viewed as an accident, doubly tragic as Lydia's parents has also been killed a car crash. But it was soon forgotten about, and the world moved on, as the world often did, occupying itself with other matters. Lydia, though, hadn't moved on. And neither had she allowed her family to.

"We simply had no idea anyone was still living there," one of the investigating police officers told Isla. "The house is set a way off the road, in't it?"

"Yes, but—"

Before Isla could say anything more, he'd interrupted her.

"People look out for one another in these parts, even in communities as rural as this. *Especially* in such communities.

It's a mystery that even her closest neighbours didn't know about her. Mind you, if you don't want no one interfering in your life, well, that's another matter, in't it? Not a lot you can do about that, really, is there?"

"Have you found her yet? Her bones?"

"If you say she's there, we will. And if we do…" His voice trailed off.

"Then you'll need to investigate me more fully. I understand that."

The officer, an older man, his face worn but kind, gave her what he clearly thought to be a reassuring smile. "I'm sure it'll be fine. You've given a statement, and there's no reason to disbelieve you. After all, it's not as if you stood anything to gain from it, is there, by burning the house down? Don't fret. It's almost New Year's Eve. You've had a terrible Christmas; you've really been through the mill. Have some fun, as you youngsters should. As I say, we'll notify you if and when a body turns up."

A terrible Christmas…not quite, but for now, her thoughts remained with Lydia. She *had* lived there all her life. Unlike the others, she was not a ghost, or a figment of Isla's imagination, no matter how wild it had run in that house that was so aptly named. A house she was driving to now in a courtesy car, her own vehicle at a local garage. They'd promised her it'd be ready for New Year's Eve morning, though. She'd offered to pay extra if necessary, and they'd agreed.

Whereabouts on the lane had Lydia ploughed into Stephen's car? Isla wondered. She rather suspected, as she passed the site of her own car crash, that it had happened there. She could find out for certain, of course, by digging deeper into the facts of the case, but actually felt no real desire to. She *knew* it had happened there, just as she knew Lydia had been if not fully alive, then *technically*, a woman who'd never embraced society but then shunned it further. She'd wanted only the past: the ghosts of those she'd loved and couldn't bear to lose, who formed the very fabric of her world. But death was coming more fully for her, and the dead too.

On reaching the driveway, she couldn't enter it by car; there was yellow caution tape across it. Snow had thawed on the roads for now, but in there, it remained.

Isla parked the car on the opposite side of the road to the entrance, and then, grabbing her rucksack from the seat beside her, got out of the car. As she shunted it on, an icy blast of wind made her shiver despite her padded jacket. She wasn't supposed to go in there – no one was except the police – but there was something she had to do. More unfinished business that needed completion.

Just before crossing the road, she looked towards the left, to where the empty house lay a mile or so up the road. Awaiting sale, apparently, the previous neighbours, a young family, having decided the idyll of rural living wasn't for them. Beyond that, *just a little beyond*, but obscured by trees, was the only other house along this track: Jessica Lockhart's, who, when Isla had failed to turn up, had phoned the agency and told them to cancel her contract with them, that she'd bloody well manage until the New Year, when she'd sort something else out. How angry Rog Ditton had been when all his calls to Isla had gone unanswered, thinking she'd changed her mind and done a runner, cleared off home or something, not bothering to check otherwise or call the police to investigate. Even now he was coming up with all the excuses under the sun about that. As for saying the house that Jessica Lockhart lived at was called Wildacre, it had been a typo he'd said. *Highacre* was where she lived.

If only she'd gone a little further that day she'd have met the real Jessica. But she'd been cold, and felt too ill, too despairing, and also concerned for her charge; that during any prolonged absence she would die alone. The latter a futile concern, in the end. Lydia would *not* have died alone; the woman had made certain of it. Perhaps, thought Isla, crossing the road, no one ever did. Not even those who thought themselves the loneliest person on earth, having run from those they loved or been abandoned. *Everyone* belonged. To someone, somewhere: to family, friends, or a lover. You could even connect with a stranger. She, Isla, had done that with Lydia. Not because she'd been sent there – she remembered how Lydia had asked her once, in a moment of lucidity, why she kept calling her Jessica, and how she'd thought nothing of it, putting it down to the woman's condition. Oh no, it was because the *Fates* had ensured it was so, or even Lydia Whittle herself, reaching out to someone, anyone – *Help! Help!* – and Isla, on some level, had heard the call. After her death, the house had had to burn, and Lydia knew that. Only then could she and her family rise fully from the ashes, cleansed.

There was no one at the house today, Isla correctly guessing that police resources wouldn't allow for monitoring 24/7, not somewhere so rural. And so, with no one to stop her, she ducked beneath the tape and continued walking up the gravel driveway. Such a long driveway, the house so far removed, as the officer had said, perhaps built by a recluse too. And, down the ages, like had called to like.

When she turned the corner, she gasped, sudden tears swelling. Such a beautiful house, *romantic*, but now it lay in

185

ruins. The fire had truly caught hold, ravaged it, a furnace that was as fierce as could be and had caused explosion after explosion.

Razed to the ground, the upper floors had collapsed completely. Perhaps, they'd never find the remains of Lydia's body, it had been truly incinerated. But even if they did, Isla wouldn't fret as the officer worried she would, for this was a death she was wholly innocent of. She'd done her best by Lydia: had stayed against all odds, holding firm even when events were at their darkest. She was proud of that.

Such an outlandish story, though, and when she'd tried to explain, to Jessica Lockhart's family that night in the car, then subsequently to the police, she'd realised how outlandish it sounded, and that she had best temper it, sticking to facts that could be easily digested. Her family, though, when she'd tried to tell them…

*Do what you came here to do, Isla. There's no need to linger.*

She'd grant herself one more look at the building, at the blackened lintels, the caved roof and collapsed chimneys, the windows which rain had once battered. When it was standing, when she'd explored, there'd been white sheets everywhere, covering all the furniture. A sign that the house was empty, perhaps, for who would live like that? No fresh food in the kitchen either, just rows of tins in cupboards, and most of them outdated. Upstairs, room after room had also lain empty. Nothing in them but the basics, all personal belongings gone.

For a moment, she hesitated, trying to work it out – as she'd done many times recently, both day and night. Had Lydia indeed been a ghost? But she had seen her so clearly! Touched her, tended to her day and night. A ghost was like the others, Amelia, Gabriel and Stephen – something that you caught out of the corner of your eye, a scampering, an echo, *a sensation.* The strangest of houses, which had supported life in all its forms, and death too. Nothing clear-cut about any of it.

Gone. And it was best it was gone, that this land lie fallow. For they *were* still here, at least three of them, their bodies deep in the ground.

But they should be together, in body, in spirit, *and* in name.

With a sigh, she turned from Wildacre, crunching again over gravel until she reached softer earth, the unkempt grass stiff as she waded through it.

There they were: the headstones, Amelia and Gabriel's; their names etched on them, and that epitaph *I Have Risen!*

She bent, feeling the coldness of the earth and the hardness of it against her knees, and traced the epitaph with her fingers, a gentle smile on her face. With a wriggle, the rucksack was off her shoulders, and on the ground beside her.

Before she grabbed it, before she rose, she reached out, tracing not the epitaph this time, but their names: a blonde-haired girl, and a boy with dark, curly hair. Beautiful children that had been loved. Perhaps…*too* loved.

She then made her way over to the unmarked grave, a mound which weeds had claimed. The police knew of these graves. The site of their burial had been formerly approved and registered, so they wouldn't be disturbed. What a grey, grey day it must have been as Lydia presided over their burial. Such a lonely day.

At the site of the mound, Isla opened her rucksack and took out what she'd been lucky enough to have had commissioned at such notice by an Alnwick craftsman. A cross. Simple. Wooden. It would rot in time, but no matter; nothing lasted for ever. Everything was fleeting. It would endure for a while yet, and that was good enough.

She placed the cross at the head of the unmarked grave, and with a hammer she'd also brought along, knocked it into place, grabbing whatever stones she could find around the grave to cement it further in as the craftsman had advised.

*Stephen Whittle,* it said. *D 1960.* Then underneath that, *Lydia Whittle, D 2020. Beloved parents of Amelia and Gabriel. Fly!*

Happy tears filled her eyes as she took a step back. If family were precious to you, you were lucky indeed. If you were precious to family, then you were blessed.

Christmas Eve night, as fire engine after fire engine arrived at the scene, she'd asked Terry and Belinda if she could borrow their mobile phone. Terry had handed his over, and they'd stepped away to give her the privacy she needed.

Her hands were shaking so much that it took several attempts to call a number she knew so well. A number that, after two years, she wished she'd called sooner.

"Mum?" she said, when it was answered. "Oh, Mum!"

She hadn't known what to expect. Instant reproach, or even worse, a frosty silence, followed by the call being ended? What she hadn't dared hope for was the joy in her mother's voice, the sheer relief.

"Isla! Oh, Isla! At last! Isla, why'd you go like you did? Just take off? We've been worried sick. We're a family, for God's sake. You belong with us."

"But Gran…" she'd managed through her tears. "Mum, I'm so sorry. You asked me to sit with her, just for a while, because you and Dad needed a break from tending to her, a night to yourselves, one night, that was all. Oh, Mum, she was asleep in bed, you know what Gran was like, she'd go flat out, it'd take an earthquake to wake her, and…and…it being Christmastime, there was stuff going on, a party. I thought…if I just showed my face for an hour or two, it'd be okay. Selfish. I always have been. But I honestly thought she'd be okay. I'd tucked her up, safe and sound. I'm sorry. So sorry. I had no idea the end was so close."

"Isla, it was bad judgement. A mistake. And yes, we have to learn from them, but we do that together. We don't run away."

"I'm sorry, Mum, so sorry."

"I know, darling. I know you are."

She'd been in charge of her gran, her *dying* gran, and she'd left her. Gran had clearly woken, perhaps even panicked, because she'd been found lying not in bed, but on the floor, her hands positioned as if reaching out, her eyes wide open. Isla had returned, after more than an hour – after more like three, after several drinks and some *relaxants* – to find her. Isla had seen the terror in her gran's eyes before the medics came, an image which seared her heart. Had heard her parents arrive too, her mother howling with grief, her father holding onto her mother but his eyes on Isla all the while. Such…disappointment there when she'd tried to explain. Her other siblings, all notified, had arrived too, their disappointment in her also plain, her sister whispering to her brother, "So fucking spoilt. She always has been."

And so, rather than face further reproach, she'd run. Left a note and gone, cut herself off, thinking it the right thing to do, the *only* option. Her family were better off without her. But she couldn't go on any more without them. Not after Wildacre.

As she continued to sob, her mother soothed her. "Isla, Isla, come home, please. We'll work through this, we will. And…you know, I think some good has come out of it, because…well, I think it could have helped you to grow, as a person, I mean. To…mature a bit. You said you went to get work as a carer, and well…that's a good thing. A great job to do. There must be so many in need out there. So many who have no one, who welcome a bit of kindness. Any kindness they can get."

"She died alone, Mum. And it was my fault."

"Gran? Oh no, no, I don't tend to think that," her mother replied.

"Huh? What do you mean?" Isla managed.

"Because…well, I'm not speaking ill of her, really I'm not, I loved Mum to bits, but she never really tried to get over her cancer once it was diagnosed. She seemed to… May God forgive me for saying this… Embrace it. Ah, she was tired, Isla, I suppose. She was old, and had simply had enough. Pops had already gone, and she never really got over that. She missed him so much. So, I have a theory. Typically, your dad thinks it's a bonkers theory, but do you want to hear it anyway?"

Isla nodded her head, *wildly* nodded. "Yes, Mum. I really do."

"It was just her time to go, and I think Dad…Pops…had come for her. *That's* why she got out of bed, why she was reaching out. Didn't you see it, love, in her eyes? There was such joy. Such…wonder. Just before that medic chap closed them."

"Joy?" And yet Isla had seen only terror. Her own, perhaps, reflected in them?

"It gives me a lot of comfort to remember that, Isla."

Isla thought for a moment and then murmured something.

"Sorry, darling? What's that?"

"I said no one ever dies alone."

"No one ever dies alone," her mother repeated, and then her voice, a wonderous thing too, added, "Yes! After Gran, after hearing so many stories from my friends since then, who've all experienced someone close to them dying, I truly believe that. There's always someone with them, and I don't just mean the living. You are coming home, aren't you, love? That's why you're phoning, isn't it? Because you've come to your senses. Oh, this is the best Christmas present ever, even to hear your voice!"

As Wildacre burned, Isla's life was resurrected.

"Yes, Mum," she'd replied. "I'll be coming home. Soon."

A rustling from behind her stopped further musings. She turned from the gravesite to check what it was. Footsteps?

What she saw was the morning sun blazing behind the building, another ring of fire around it. It glowed. And it was golden. Not blackened at all, no longer a husk. Something that had once been – and still was, in its own way – glorious.

Had the sun highlighted something else too, at what had been an upstairs window? She narrowed her eyes as she hurried closer. It was a figure of some sort, the merest outline, faint, hazy, wispy. That of a young woman, as far as Isla could tell, a familiar young woman, a man beside her, and two others, a girl and a boy.

The Whittles. Standing there, just them. Imagination. This time it had to be. Something in her was needing to see them the way they could have been. Nonetheless, she lifted her hand, and smiled as she waved.

It was the girl who returned the gesture. Amelia.

And then the sun faded, clouds having blown across its path, perhaps, and what had been at the window – Lydia's bedroom, she realised – was no more.

But something in Isla remained ablaze.

*You have to bring light to the season…*

They – the Whittles – had done that for her. Dispensed with the darkness.

A new year, a new start, in the arms of her family. She was a woman who'd matured, as her mother had said, who still had a long road ahead, but who'd never take any day of it for granted, who would meet life head on, love and love fearlessly. There may be darkness in amongst the light – more guilt, lows and highs, all of it inevitable – but with Lydia in her heart, a woman who'd called her an angel, she could do it. Believe in herself again. Because Lydia, she was an angel too.

A cold blast causing more shivers, Isla retraced her steps along the gravel path, past the house, and the three stone urns, and she *flew* out of Wildacre.

# A note from the author

As much as I love writing, building a relationship with readers is even more exciting! I occasionally send newsletters with details on new releases, special offers and other bits of news relating to the Psychic Surveys series as well as all my other books. If you'd like to subscribe, sign up here!

## www.shanistruthers.com